GREG WAITED UNTIL SHE RE... <del>S0-BOD-295</del> alley, then with split-second timing yanked Annie around the corner and into his arms. . . .

Emotions raced across her face faster than a summer storm—shock, anger, readiness to fight. Then she recognized him. A touch of alarm widened her eyes, a hint of happy surprise colored her cheeks. Beneath it all, undeniable currents of sexual excitement simmered.

She'd been tempting him all week long. But this wasn't a joke or a game. He knew what he'd been waiting for. He kissed her. Hard.

Annie closed her eyes and shivered with the pleasure of it. This kiss was no tease. It wasn't angry, unless a badger teased out of its hole was angry. It wasn't demanding, unless the absolute need of a man for a woman was demanding. And it wasn't dangerous, unless falling in love was dangerous. . . .

WHAT ARE *LOVESWEPT* ROMANCES?

They are stories of true romance and touching emotion. We believe those two very important ingredients are constants in our highly sensual and very believable stories in the LOVESWEPT line. Our goal is to give you, the reader, stories of consistently high quality that may sometimes make you laugh, sometimes make you cry, but are always fresh and creative and contain many delightful surprises within their pages.

Most romance fans read an enormous number of books. Those they truly love, they keep. Others may be traded with friends and soon forgotten. We hope that each LOVESWEPT romance will be a treasure—a "keeper." We will always try to publish

LOVE STORIES YOU'LL NEVER FORGET
BY AUTHORS YOU'LL ALWAYS REMEMBER

The Editors

DANCING
ON THE EDGE

TERRY
LAWRENCE

BANTAM BOOKS

NEW YORK · TORONTO · LONDON · SYDNEY · AUCKLAND

For my Dad

DANCING ON THE EDGE
A Bantam Book / September 1993

*If you would be interested in receiving protective vinyl covers for your
Loveswept books, please write to this address for information:*

Loveswept
Bantam Books
P.O. Box 985
Hicksville, NY 11802

ISBN 0-553-44305-4

Published simultaneously in the United States and Canada

ONE

Butterflies the size of pterodactyls.

Annie Oakley Cartwright wiped a sweaty palm down the side of her jeans, minimizing a case of nerves by imagining her fear flapping its way across the prehistoric Arizona landscape.

Her mind temporarily at ease, she concentrated on her body. Her skin tingled. Her nerves sang. She liked that. She savored it. Nothing made her feel more alive, nothing. A solid adrenaline buzz gave her the focused feeling a stuntwoman needed before doing something dangerous.

So why this untimely attack of nerves? Her "To Do" list was really very simple: (a) meet Greg Ford, (b) jump out of a moving car.

At least she had experience with one.

"Now, Annie," she muttered, "you've jumped out of cars, helicopters, and burning buildings. You've been thrown by broncos, mean-tempered horses, and a hornet-stung pony. You can handle Greg Ford."

She'd been eight when that pony had thrown her. She'd been falling and getting right back up ever since. This was her first full motion picture after two years of TV cop shows and one-shot stunts. Impressing the stunt coordinator meant everything. That she would be impressed *by* him had her quaking in her size-six cowboy boots.

Greg Ford had the toughest reputation in the business and, as a direct consequence, the safest record. Annie might equate risk taking with being really alive, but she prided herself on never doing any stunt stupidly or halfheartedly.

She thought it out thoroughly, *then* she jumped. With both feet. The Good Lord help the man who told her there was anything in this world she couldn't do.

Annie chuckled at her own silent pep talk. Her heels scraped the baked earth as she strode toward the location trailer. Overhead, the merciless midsummer sun beat down on Monument Valley. The twenty-foot trailer looked like a Tinkertoy of the gods. A canvas awning unfurled outside it. In the shade, half a dozen men stood around a folding table.

Annie politely elbowed her way into the circle. "Mr. Ford?"

"Greg." He said it as if it were an order.

She nodded, gripped his hand firmly, and looked him in the eye. Nerves, all hers, zinged up her arm.

"Good to meet you, Greg. Annie Cartwright reporting for work."

The man should have been an actor, she thought instantly. Those eyes, that squint. Cheekbones like that didn't give a man's face much room to stretch. In fact, taut described him all over, from the grim line of his mouth to the lingering ache of his handshake. He looked carved out of mesa sandstone. Apparently his personality was just as unyielding.

"Hold on," he said without further ado, turning a level gaze on a young stuntman standing six feet away.

The boy swallowed audibly. He reminded Annie of a bronco rider gripping the saddle moments before the horn sounded and the bull jumped out of the chute. Apparently, Greg Ford was about to jump down his throat.

That would be some mouthful.

Greg was a head taller than Annie, his shoulders nearly a saddle-width wider. His hair was tumbleweed brown, his eyes prairie-sky blue. She counted three scars, each of them enhancing his gritty, rugged brand of masculinity. As hard as a fall from a mustang on a dry day, she thought.

Obviously the stuntman had screwed up. Annie decided then and there that the next person to do it wouldn't be her. There was no hotdogging on Greg's films. He tolerated mistakes the way a rattler tolerates getting stepped on.

"What have you got to say for yourself?" he demanded.

The silence stretched like the stark afternoon shadows. Thumbs stuck in his back pants pockets, the unlucky stuntman shifted from one foot to the other.

"You got any idea what your—your mess-up is going to cost this film?" Greg asked.

"No, sir."

The cleaned-up curse was for her benefit. Annie would have to tell Greg the nicety wasn't necessary. She'd been around men all her life; four-letter words were a given. Judging from the resentment burning its way to the tips of the young man's ears, *Ford* had become the newest four-letter word in the English language.

Greg barked another command. "You got any idea what a day of filming costs?"

"No, sir."

"You got any idea what your life is worth?"

"Not a plugged nickel right about now," the young man ventured.

"Bull!" Greg's thundering denunciation quickly subsided to a rumble. "Your life, son, is worth ten of these lousy action pics. You're the one treating it like a pile of—"

"I only wanted—"

"To hotdog it and show us all up. Prove what a whiz kid you are and what beat-up old has-beens *we* are."

As far as Annie could judge, Greg was no more than thirty-eight. The boy, though, was closer to twenty. A kid with a lot to prove—and nothing to say.

"You're suspended," Greg announced. "You take

the day off and think about whether you want your name on the stunt credits of this film or a tombstone. If you'd rather have the glory, get off my picture."

The young man turned on his heel and headed for a motorcycle.

"And don't start that thing with the cameras rolling!"

He kicked dirt and kept going.

"And wear a helmet," Greg said half to himself. "What're you lookin' at?"

The men surrounding the table let out slow breaths and low whistles. "You're gettin' soft, boss."

Annie peeked at Greg's flinty glare and sincerely doubted that.

An older man nudged her, tilting his head toward the retreating stuntman. "Damn fool practically got his head cut off sliding his cycle under a semi. Lapse in concentration."

"Ah."

At the sound of her voice, the other men turned to her one by one. Greg Ford flipped the pages of a script. Like the temperature rising on a thermometer, Annie's tension rose one degree for each second she waited for him to look up. Her heartbeat picked up. Beads of sweat glistened between her breasts. Her knees went a little weak.

Darn, this was fun.

Annie Oakley, you are perverse! Nevertheless, the daring, roughhouse side of her almost wished she'd done something to make him mad. Going toe-to-toe with Greg Ford might be worth the shouting. Before this picture was over, she promised herself she'd do just that.

If she got the job, that was.

"They tell me you're good," he said.

"I hope you'll be satisfied. With my work, I mean." Annie listened to the men snicker and tried to stop the blood from rising to her cheeks. She gave up and laughed along with them.

Greg Ford didn't crack a smile. "This is your first full picture?"

"I hope so."

"You hoping to get my attention by pulling crazy stunts like Jackson over there?"

"I'm here to replace Julie McLean."

He winced. The others immediately quieted down. Uh-oh, Annie thought. She'd already stepped in it and she didn't even know what it was. She only knew she'd replaced a stuntwoman injured in a fall from a horse.

Greg tapped the eraser end of a pencil against the map. "I hope you do a better job."

The hair on the back of her neck bristled. This work was hard enough for women without Julie taking the blame for some crazy horse's mistake. Annie crossed her arms; her eyes narrowed. "I know Julie McLean, Mr. Ford. She's a precise, accomplished, levelheaded—"

He slapped the script onto the table. Annie jumped. "We loaded her in the air-ambulance yesterday. What do you think I did, chew her out as they were hoisting her up?"

Nose to nose with Greg Ford already. She was going to have to be more careful about what she wished for.

"The horse is named Dickens," he declared. "He is one too. Julie was so busy wrestling him for the reins, she missed her mark. When the planted charges went off, the horse shied and rolled on her. She's lucky her leg was all she broke."

Annie resisted the urge to shift from foot to foot like that forlorn stuntman. "I'm sorry," she said. "I misunderstood. I guess it's okay."

"Mistakes are *never* okay." His voice barely rose above the whisper of the hot breeze blowing dust across their boots. "If the job's done right, no one gets hurt."

She suddenly understood a lot more than his words. He wasn't worried about everything going right because he said so, or because his reputation was on the line, or because they were over budget and behind schedule.

He'd chewed that boy out because he cared. His voice turned to sand and his hands to fists when he talked about Julie McLean, because he cared. Annie saw it etched in the hard planes of his face; the blame and guilt were practically eating him up.

"You feel responsible for the accident," she said softly.

"I *am* responsible."

Gazing into eyes the color of the sky at high noon,

Annie thought she'd never met a more fascinating man. His toughness was genuine, hard as rock. But the heart inside was bigger than this whole outdoors. And, despite one ear-sore, saddle-sore cycle jockey speeding his Harley toward the horizon, every man at this table knew it.

Her respect for Greg leapt right past the rumors and straight into reality. A smile spread over her face like a sunbeam. She leaned forward and gave him a quick hug. "I think I'm going to like working with you."

He jumped back as if he'd been snakebit. "What?" His scowl made her smile even wider.

"This is going to be fun."

"Stunts aren't *fun*."

"Oh yeah?" Edging up to the table, she bumped him with a wicked wiggle of her hip. "Tell me what I'm supposed to do and we'll see about that. Boss."

Set back on his heels, Greg glared at six men, none of whom could hide a grin although every last one of them was trying.

"Go ahead, boss," one of them chuckled. "Tell her what you two are gonna do."

He paused. For a very very long time. "We'll refilm the horse gag later in the shoot. We've got another stunt set for today."

"What is it?"

Annie thought she heard his teeth grind. Her heart sank. She *needed* this job.

She knew her slight body, tight jeans, small chest,

and five-foot-three-inch frame weren't very impressive. Standing beside Greg Ford, she didn't look big enough or strong enough. She knew it. He knew it. But gymnastics and martial arts, aerobics and stunt training, hell, just plain cussedness made up for a lot.

"Annie," her daddy had told her, "you'll be proving yourself every single day in this business and that's a fact. Anyone gives you any trouble, you just lift your chin and look down that skinny nose of yours at 'em. That'll make 'em think twice. If not, switch your hair a bit; that'll distract 'em."

It grated on her pride like sand between her teeth, but she did as her daddy suggested. She put one hand on her hip, looked right up at Greg Ford, and swished her ivory-blond hair back over her shoulder. "I can do anything you want, Mr. Ford. Anything."

The low whistle came from someone else. The dare remained in Annie's eyes.

Greg looked her up and down, spending more time on her eyes than her size. Questions got answered without ever being asked. "The stunt is you and me together in the backseat of a car, rolling down a mountainside."

She pulled her mouth into a flat-line smile, hoping to camouflage a gulp. "The backseat," she repeated.

"It starts out as a love scene. Then it turns dangerous."

She believed that.

He immediately picked up her apprehension—and the cause. She'd jumped from moving cars before. But the very idea of "doing it" with Greg Ford sent her blood pressure jetting into the endless blue sky.

"Think you can handle that?" He meant could she handle him.

She flexed her fingers where they rested on her hip. "I can handle it. I might even enjoy it."

Electricity crackled between them. She felt a different kind of edgy now—the kind that didn't flap its wings and fly away. It didn't help that tension radiated off *him* in heat waves.

"We walk through it, then we do it," he said.

"Gotcha."

"Any questions, you ask, don't assume."

She wanted to ask if his voice always rasped like sand pitting stone, or if it had anything to do with the sudden nearly tactile awareness between them.

His next question brought her up short. "Are you scared?"

She swallowed dust and dry air. "A little."

"Good. Gut-check honesty is rule one around here. Any worries, doubts, inklings, premonitions, nerves, you come to me. Okay, guys, let's walk her through it."

He hefted a stopwatch, thoughtfully scraping his thumb over the scuffed casing. Before she could follow the crew toward a sedan parked in the sun, he stopped her with a handful of softly spoken words. "Will you come to me, Annie?"

Deeply afraid that the answer was in her eyes, she turned to him. He was the kind of man a woman *would* go to if she was worried. Exactly the kind of man who scared the heck out of her. A hotdogging devil-may-care stuntman could get someone killed. A concerned, caring one could break her heart. Stunt work was infinitely safer. "If I have a problem with a stunt, Mr. Ford, you'll be the first to know."

"Let's do it."

"Let's."

Gut-check honesty or no, she kept this set of butterflies entirely to herself.

Two sweating beer cans anchored the unrolled map of the east side of the mountain. The stopwatch sat atop a second-by-second breakdown of the stunt. A shooting script, well thumbed and curling at the edges, flapped open as a gust of wind caught it. The cover beat against the table.

Annie flashed glances at Greg as he explained the stunt for the third time.

Okay, so he had a reputation for perfection. In stunt work, near misses trailed a person like the tip of a whip. With Julie's fall, the whip had finally snapped. Greg couldn't have acted more guilty, more haunted.

"Do you need to go over it again?" His tone was gruff, the intent gentle.

Nevertheless, Annie hurriedly crossed her arms and hid a smile behind a hand. She shook her head. A strangled "Nope" escaped her lips.

"You sure?" He was so sincere.

She glanced at the other men for help. They looked away. "It's fine, Greg."

"I want you to be clear on absolutely everything before we get in that car."

"Greg." She put her hand on his arm. He was a dear, dear man and she admired him more by the minute. "If you explain it to me one more time, I'm going to know the aerodynamics, the thermodynamics, and every other dynamic involved in this stunt. I understand. Really."

Lightly lifting the pencil out of his hand, she repeated his instructions, tracing the route he'd described. "We get in the backseat, replaying the moves the actress and actor did in the love scene. Then you push the gear shift into neutral. Our motion starts the car rolling down this twisting mountain road. You reach over the seat to steer; we scrape off the mountain wall a couple times. The car careens through a rotted guardrail, plunges five hundred feet down a cliff, and explodes. We jump and roll three seconds before that happens. We do it in one take."

Simple. Or it would have been if he hadn't stepped up close enough to stop a whisper. He lifted a handful of loose shimmery hair fluttering across her breast and sifted it through his fingers. "Silk."

Each strand became a live wire attached to a nerve ending. Annie's heartbeat tripped and stuttered. A misty quivery sensation ran rivulets between her shoulder blades. She chased it away. One minute he hovered over her like a mother hen, the next the man/woman connection sizzled between them. "You want to check my teeth next? I feel as if I'm being bet on in the Derby."

The other men laughed. Greg didn't.

"I'm betting my life on you, Silk. That's not something I take lightly *or* do with strangers."

She lifted her face to him. "Getting horizontal in back seats isn't something I take lightly either. Or do with strangers."

Greg gave her a wind-scoured grimace. "I take my work seriously."

"So I noticed." She held her ground, aware of something new in his eyes, a grudging willingness to give her a chance. Her heart soared.

"All right, Silk. But you tie that hair back before we get in the car."

"Will do."

They rehearsed every detail. They crawled in and out of the car, slamming doors while he grilled her on her part, peppering her with rapid-fire questions. Annie thought that if he'd ever smiled, it must have been in another lifetime; he was all business now.

A production assistant tiptoed to the edge of the encampment and whined, "Are we going to get this show on the road anytime soon? Like before sundown?"

Uncomfortably close in the sedan's backseat, Annie saw a vein beat on the side of Greg's corded neck.

The assistant stuck his balding head in the open window of the car, knocking his baseball cap askew.

"The director's yelling holy hell about delays, Ford. You know that."

Judging from the way the other stuntmen took to staring at their boots and squinting off toward the horizon, everybody on the set knew it.

"We're just about ready," Greg replied.

"'Just about' don't fry the bacon."

"We'll be there."

The assistant smiled tightly and spoke into a walkie-talkie. "He says they'll be there."

No one in the crew moved until the crackling response faded away. Someone spit a stream of tobacco juice in the dirt.

Greg automatically extended a hand to help Annie out of the backseat. "Ready?"

"As ready as I'll ever be." She laughed. She was as ready as a hot-wired car, in more ways than one.

An hour in close quarters with Greg Ford and her body felt every impress of his hands, every unintentional bumping of knees and thighs. The too-near breathing of a man's mouth beside her ear left her with a lingering achy arousal. She tucked back a strand of hair, surreptitiously tugging her earlobe as if to signal her brain, *Enough of that.*

"Costume brought over your outfit." Greg nodded toward a bundle of white satin folded on the map table.

"Thanks."

"You change your clothes in there."

Annie started briskly for the trailer, relieved to be released from the stifling confines of the car, those buttery leather seats that slid against skin and smelled so good. The kind a man and woman could make the most of.

Greg's hand caught her arm and she let out a tiny gasp. "Remember, if you're scared, you tell me. That's a rule."

He'd misinterpreted her attack of nerves. Just because she scurried away from him at warp speed was no reason for him to think she was scared.

Why should she be? He hadn't taken advantage of their close quarters to put his hands anywhere they didn't absolutely have to be. It was *her* responsibility to get her mind out of an R-rated movie and into real life. "I've been in this business awhile, Mr. Ford. I can do a jump and roll."

He squinted so hard, she thought he was going to curse or spit. "*Mister*. Makes me sound like somebody's father."

"My daddy says you're one of the best."

"Rusty Cartwright?"

"Mm-hmm." She always stood up straighter when her daddy's name was mentioned. He was nearly a legend in this business.

"Quite a horseman in his day," Greg said.

"Certainly was."

"Julie McLean was good too."

"Meaning?"

He put his hands on his hips and fixed her with the kind of stare a man might train on a brick wall coming at him at sixty miles an hour, coolly calculating the split second before he hit the brakes. "I designed that stunt. Somebody got hurt. The next one's even more dangerous. If you don't want to work with me, walk now and nobody'll hold it against you. I've done everything I can to make it work, but I can't guarantee—"

She shook her head. "Life doesn't come with guarantees."

"I just wanted you to know I'll be on top of this all the way."

Images of him on top of her made her cheeks flush. She had to break this tension between them or they'd never be able to concentrate on the stunt. She leaned toward him, confiding in a low smoky voice, "That's kind of what I was afraid of."

For one brief moment his eyes actually sparkled. He tilted his head and gave her a calculating look. "Was I getting to you back there?"

"Oh, I wouldn't say that. I might *think* it, but I wouldn't say it."

He threw his head back and laughed.

Annie immediately regretted the fact that she hadn't tickled him at least once, hadn't eased away some of the tension coiling around him like a hungry python until now. He wanted her to know he'd put his best into designing this stunt. She wanted him to loosen up and enjoy it a little.

"What would you do if I did walk out on a stunt?" she asked, cockier than a near rookie had any right to be. "What would you do without me?"

"Put one of the men in a dress. That's how they used to do it."

"Them? In the backseat of that?" She gave a hoot of laughter. "No way. Uh-uh. You need me, Ford, admit it." She flounced toward the trailer.

Greg dogged her heels.

Annie grabbed the dress off the map table as she sashayed by, then whirled on him. Their chests collided.

"Sorry." He touched the brim of the dusty black cowboy hat he'd picked up from the same table, slanting it over his eyes.

"Do you get this worked up about every stuntman on your crew or just the women?"

"It's my job."

"One hundred percent safety is impossible."

"I know." The words chipped away at him like a sculptor working stone. "But I can't—"

"Guarantee it. Don't worry. Mom always said I had more lives than a bad-luck cat."

"You don't have to risk one with me."

"Don't I?" She sidled up to him, lowering her voice to a husky imitation of Marlene Dietrich. "I think you're one of the riskiest men I've ever met."

She got the husk right, but she forgot the German accent.

Greg took every word at face value. He swallowed. His eyes darkened as if a cloud had crossed the sun.

There were no clouds, Annie thought, not in the sky, not in his eyes. Maybe it was an eclipse. One of those rare moments when the planets lined up, worlds collided, the earth moved . . .

"Hey, boss," one of the men yelled. "They got your costume over here."

The spell broke. She swatted Greg's thigh with the dress she clutched, covering up her breathlessness with a laugh. "Scoot. I've got to change my clothes."

Annie entered the trailer. On tiptoe, she peeked out the window. His head was bowed, his shoulders raised. His heels thudded deliberately against the ground. She hadn't meant to make him *more* tense.

She pursed her lips and whistled as loudly as she could, a warbling version of "Falling in Love Again."

As if stung by a horsefly, his hand clamped the back of his neck. He gave it a good hard squeeze. Inch by inch he turned, squinting in the direction of the trailer.

Annie ducked. Life was too short to be wound that tight. The man needed to laugh at least once more before the century ran out. "And you're the woman for the job," she muttered to herself.

Hey, why not? She'd never turned down a dare before.

TWO

The musky aroma of old cigarette smoke stuck to the gloomy walnut paneling in the trailer. Annie let her nose adjust. She had five motionless seconds to concentrate on stopping the shaking in her legs.

She'd always been blessed with confidence, the plain stubborn kind of all-out ego she could flick on like a light switch. When she took on a job, she absolutely refused to consider the down side. Thinking about failure meant a person expected to fail.

Live it all. That was her motto. At fifteen she would have had it tattooed on her shoulder if her daddy hadn't hauled her out of that tattoo parlor. She met life head on, always had. A brother dead at twenty-two and a father's career cut short by arthritis from too many injuries, had taught her to walk right up to life and hug it close. Nobody ever said it was going to last.

Greg Ford, on the other hand, seemed intent on

out-thinking life at every disastrous turn. Though not a bad philosophy for a stunt coordinator, it made for a nerveracking life.

"If he held the reins any tighter, his knuckles would turn white," Annie muttered.

After a day's acquaintance, she liked and respected him enough to want to help him out. To shake him up a bit. Take some of the starch out of his shorts.

Chuckling, she slipped on the gear she'd brought. First came a flesh-colored bodysuit designed to protect her skin when she hit the pavement. Next came elbow pads and knee pads. She buttoned the fabric-covered buttons on the slinky gown Costuming had delivered, a floor-length swath of white satin.

Annie briefly wondered what the heroine of this picture was doing wearing this getup in Monument Valley. But making sense out of action-pic scripts wasn't her business. Making sense of her emotions before a stunt was.

The fabric skimmed the inside of her arm where Greg had touched her moments ago. *Silk*, he'd said. One raspy word reduced her to palpitations.

That was life, too, she thought with a wry smile. The sweet sexy part. A smart woman could enjoy it without succumbing to it. She had a job to do. "If life is brief, movie-set romances can be counted in nanoseconds."

Her hair shimmied as she ran a brush through it, tying it back the way Belinda Saint wore it in the upcoming scene. The way Greg had asked her to. She gulped a handful of water from the tap and patted her mouth dry, then she closed her eyes and took stock.

The butterflies were still there, 747s now, beating out a message she couldn't ignore. Getting horizontal in the backseat of a car with Greg Ford would be more dangerous than any special effects gimmick.

"Talk about feeling alive!"

Mid-afternoon on a dusty mountain road. Sand pelted the windows, urged on by a scouring wind. Annie and Greg sweltered in the car waiting for the camera-rolling signal.

"Ready?" Greg asked.

Annie nodded. She took a deep breath, gazing into eyes whose edges were carved with gullies of deep-set wrinkles.

"He wants us to do what the actors did, so the shots match." Greg meant the director, Lucas Stone. "They'll intercut the long shots of the car with the interiors from Belinda's scene."

Belinda Saint was the star of the film. She and Nicholas Strand had spent three days in the backseat of this car working through a love scene.

More like a torture scene, Annie thought, squirming in a ladylike way to get some more room. "Fine," she said. "Whatever they need for the shot."

"That means kissing."

"Does it?" Her lips tingled where she licked them, as if she'd tasted something spicy and it still burned.

"You can't cut from two people grappling in a backseat to a long shot of two heads sitting there chatting," Greg explained unnecessarily. "We need to, um . . ."

"Did I say I minded?" Her chin came up.

A thin smile creased his face. "Let's do it." He glanced at a crumpled piece of legal pad in his hand, a list of the moves they'd have to make to simulate the love scene. "I'm usually a little more spontaneous."

A joke! Annie practically threw her arms around him and kissed him. "Trying to put me at ease?" she teased.

"Are you?"

"As at ease as a woman can be in the backseat of a car with a strange man who's about to kiss her." She batted her lashes and puckered up.

Greg shook his head and laughed, a chuckling rumble that reminded her of distant thunder. "I thought you'd have more nerves."

"Where I come from, this *is* some nerve." She tucked her fingers behind the lapel of his tuxedo, running her other palm down the front of his ruffled shirt. "Nice duds."

He crooked his mouth in another smile. It didn't match the cautiousness in his eyes. "I hoped you'd like it."

"What do you think the plot of this thing is, anyway? A woman in an evening gown, a man in a tux, a Mercedes on a mountainside in Arziona. It's a long way to travel to go parking."

"Maybe her dad has a shotgun."

"Maybe."

Annie felt the tiniest bit of relaxation go through him. He'd checked his crib sheet no more than five times in the last ten seconds. It was an improvement.

She glimpsed fragments of sentences there, printed in blocky black handwriting: "Two heads in the back-seat window. Kiss. Lie down."

"How romantic," she quipped.

He looked out the window once more. Annie knew the minute the signal came by the way his body tensed.

"Do we kiss now?"

His eyes locked with hers. He ran his hand over her hair, a gentle stroke—not so gentle that she mistook the power of his fingers curling around the back of her head and lifting her face to his. "I think we do."

They began. Clothes whispered against clothes. He took it all so seriously, so carefully. As far as Annie was concerned, until the car started rolling down the mountainside, the rest was purely playacting.

She slipped into a Southern accent as outrageous as her teasing. "You have done this before, haven't you, suh?"

"I have years of experience." He brushed his lips over hers. He meant stunt work.

She meant business. "Then I'm perfectly safe with you?"

"Perfectly."

She pouted. "I was afraid of that. My daddy said—"

"Your daddy isn't here and if he was—" He didn't

finish the sentence. After what happened next, Annie got the idea it would've had something to do with horsewhipping.

Greg slid his arms around her. He seductively brushed his lips across hers. Seductive because he withheld that little bit, taking it to the edge of his self-control, and hers. Seductive because he wasn't entirely faking.

He nipped her lower lip with his, never using his teeth, never opening his mouth except to tell her which way to lean, where to put her arms. Then he slipped his hand under her behind and pulled her closer.

Fireflies danced on her skin, dust devils in the desert heat. Her tongue wet her lips, accidentally touching the corner of his. His breath smelled of peppermint and the cigarette he'd half smoked and then impatiently tossed aside before they'd gotten in the car.

She wanted to ask if they could open a window—all these quick little breaths weren't getting any air into her lungs—but before she could, he murmured a hoarse command. "Put your head back." He spread her hair on the rear window ledge. Just because he was supposed to didn't lessen the effect—not when she caught the reverent expression on his face.

His other hand curved around her ribcage, carefully avoiding the delicate underside of her breast, the one that teased his thumb every time she moved. "Does your heart always beat this fast?" he asked.

"A woman's heart beats fast in a situation like this or she's clinically dead."

His chuckle went through her like a cool glass of water. She wanted to hear it again.

He slid her farther down the seat. The world tilted. It was in the script; she had to lie down to get out of the shot. He had to sink down on top of her.

"Uh, Greg? I've heard of working under somebody, but this is ridiculous." Weak joke.

He laughed anyway. Maneuvering, he kicked the side door with his boot. "Damn these foreign cars." His jaw went rigid. "Do you have to wriggle so much?"

"It's not so easy in a backseat."

"Just don't say it's hard."

She laughed, but that made her body ripple under his.

He cursed softly. Carefully, very very carefully, he lowered himself on her. The muscles in his arms bunched as he held himself off by scant inches. "Know what comes next?"

"I wouldn't be a woman if I didn't."

His mouth crooked. Transferring all his weight to one arm, he skimmed ivory hair off her neck. No camera would ever catch that tender touch. Her eyes fluttered shut. "You don't have to act here," he murmured. "We're out of the shot."

Her eyes opened. Who'd said anything about acting?

"Half a minute and we get it rolling."

As far as she was concerned, things were moving plenty fast already.

Their breaths mingled. Somebody swallowed. Annie turned her head, opening her mouth to steal a breath. "Greg?"

"Silk." This time he meant the skin beneath her ear.

Lord, that felt good. Fiery little sparks raced up and down her throat as he traced it with the slightly callused pad of his index finger. "They can't see us," she said, the words eddying out on a whisper. She meant he didn't *have* to play the scene move for move. In this context it sounded like permission.

She tried to sit up. "What I meant—"

He caught her before she got in the shot. "Whoa, I know what you meant." His knee prodded the inside of her thigh, unintentionally setting off a jolt of intense arousal. He knelt on the floor with the other knee, glancing down at the scuffed old stopwatch. He winked at her. "Lucky charm. Don't tell."

"How much time do we have?"

"Honey, a lifetime wouldn't be enough for this."

He was trying to defuse the situation with his own understated humor. She was trying to keep her breasts from brushing his chest as she laughed.

His expression grew serious. "About thirty seconds. Got that?"

Thirty seconds, she thought. Shouldn't be hard. Just lie there with Greg Ford on top of her and count the seams in the ceiling while he toyed absently with strands of her hair.

For once in her life, Annie understood why love scenes got out of hand, why movie-star marriages were as unpredictable as lava flows. Something flowed in her. It started with his lips brushing the side of her neck unnecessarily; it pooled downward, like an undiscovered pond in a mountain cave. The riptide sensations coursing through her, the confusion, the surprising doubt, were hard enough for her to handle. They couldn't possibly be mirrored in his eyes.

They were.

"This is crazy," he murmured.

She nodded, afraid to acknowledge what they both felt. Afraid to let it go unexplored. Life was too short—

"Silk?"

"Yes?" She hesitated long enough to get lost in his eyes again.

He cursed. He looked at the time. He looked at her mouth and paused, his breath warm on her face. "Hell."

His lips crushed hers. She gripped him to her. His hips prodded the softness of her belly with an unmistakable hardness.

She couldn't say what part of him touched her first. What touched her *most* was the way he hesitated before the next kiss, silently asked.

She lifted her head. She opened to him.

As hot as the desert around them, his tongue reminded her of the searing taste of danger or sweet drugging poison. His hands were rough, quick, molding her to him, tracing the fall of her waist, flattening beneath her shoulder blades to press her to him.

This wasn't acting. Nor was it any child's idea of

let's pretend. His kiss held all the desperate need of a man who hadn't tasted love in a long, long time. Not just sex, the real thing, the rare thing.

Annie wanted to give it to him.

She gasped and tore her mouth away. "Wait."

"Too much?"

"Too everything."

They paused. She watched a flicker of emotion darken his face. He glanced at the time. He *apologized*. "Sorry, Annie, I—"

"Don't." She touched his face, her fingertips covering his lips. For a moment, she couldn't bear to hear it. How could she blame him for anything as pure and stark as that naked need? No script-written lines, no movie-star come-ons, this was man and woman stuff, as real as life on the edge. "Being alive isn't something you apologize for," she said, then smiled. "Now we can concentrate on the scene."

Breath rushed out of him. "Right."

His boot kicked the gear shift between the front seats. He meant it to. He buried his face in her hair, his breathing harsh and short. "This is it."

The car shuddered and rocked underneath them, gravity beginning its tug on the downward slope. The wheels began to hum. The clatter of gravel and the corduroy of a rutted road testified to their gathering speed.

"Go!"

They broke apart as the car careened down the mountain road. Greg lunged for the gearshift. A sharp sickening bend in the road threw him off. He got one hand around it while the other clutched the steering wheel. His sure grip was all that prevented them from hurtling over the edge.

Working the hand brake to slow them when needed, he steered toward the right. Annie's side of the car scraped the mountain's stone wall with a banshee's shriek. That bought them a handful of seconds until an outcropping of rock forced them back out to the center of the road. The rumble of frantic acceleration grew to a roar.

"Get ready to jump," he shouted.

Annie's hand was slick on the door handle. She grasped it tightly, gauging the speed of the pavement whizzing by. Planting her feet on the mat, she put her shoulder to the door.

"Jump!"

She yanked the handle. Nothing happened. "It's stuck!"

Straight ahead, the road curved sharply, then ended in nothing but air and sky and a guardrail purposely designed not to hold them.

Greg shoved her back against the seat. Bracing against his own door, he kicked hers. It popped open. Air rushed by. Annie didn't stop to think. She dove and rolled. Hitting the ground hard, she spun, feeling the jagged stones scrape and claw, eager to rend any unprotected flesh.

After dizzying seconds, she came to a stop, her stomach lurching, her lungs aching. The air was torn by the unmistakable screech of a knife honed by a grindstone. Metal scraped metal. Around the curve, the guardrail gave way with an ugly tearing sound. Tires screamed as they left the pavement.

Eerie and absolute silence followed. Without being fully aware of it, Annie counted the seconds. She heard the far-off crash, the accordion crumpling of metal, the inevitable explosion.

Her ears buzzed, then sang. The *swoop swoop swoop* of a helicopter approached. A cold sweat broke out on her skin. She looked up to see a man leaning out the chopper's open doorway, a loudspeaker in his hand.

"Cut!" the director yelled.

Annie leapt to her feet and ran.

Around the corner at the end of the guardrail, on the loose gravel shoulder where the road ended and God's own sky began, Greg gingerly tested his limbs. Feet, ankles, and knees all worked, nothing dislocated or sprained. It was a minor exercise he went through after every completed stunt. And a meaningless one, considering the fact he'd stopped three feet short of a five-hundred-foot drop-off. He was alive. How hurt could he be?

"Takes a licking and keeps on ticking," he muttered, clutching his lucky stopwatch.

Suddenly his brain kicked into gear. "Annie!" He strained to sit up, then thought better of it. She'd gotten out, he knew that. He'd have to trust her to take a fall. He'd almost taken a bigger one.

The damn door stuck! The sideswipe against the mountain wall must have jammed it. Another near miss. Another lucky break. If he didn't know better, he'd blame the stunt coordinator.

He ran a hand over his face and cursed. "You sorry son of a bitch, you *are* the stunt coordinator."

"Boss! Boss, you okay?" Bill Broderick and Jack Cronyn braked the Jeep to a halt a few feet away.

Greg sat up fast, flinching at a back spasm. He and the hot tub had an appointment tonight. He dusted off the seat of the tuxedo as he got to his feet. "Just great. How's the girl?"

"The stunt*woman* is fine. You're the one who almost took the high dive."

"A high dive for a lowlife. Sounds fitting."

"I'll say."

Greg looked up at the sound of a feminine voice. If the bottom hadn't dropped out of his stomach five minutes ago when that door had burst open at the last second, it would've dropped now.

She came at him with her hair unraveled from its blue satin ribbon. Streaks of sun danced among the white-gold strands, and an indulgent smile curled her lips. She wasn't hurt. Good. He couldn't deal with hurting another woman. Not after Julie McLean.

Not after Pam.

Greg bit down on a piece of rock and wished he'd spit the grit out of his mouth before she got there. He wiped the bloody scrape on his palm against the front of his tuxedo shirt. He idly examined the scratch. He didn't see her coming until she was almost on top of him.

"Whooeee!" She wrapped her arms and legs around him, damn near toppling them over the cliff. "Wasn't that fantastic?"

"What?" He tried to get his hands on her waist. He got a handful of breast instead. His hand snapped back as if burned.

She laughed, grabbing his wrists, tugging him toward her while she danced a Texas two-step. "Come on!"

"What in tarnation—?"

"Dance with me."

"She's flipped," he said to the crew members.

Annie smiled blissfully. "How many chances do you get to literally dance on the edge? This is it. This is as close as we get."

"Got that right." He stepped back. The world fell away. Five hundred feet of nothing and a plume of smoke from a burning car. "You want me to be happy about almost going over that?"

"*Almost* is the operative word." She wanted him to laugh, to celebrate, to *live*. But she couldn't explain it, not in those words.

Greg turned his back on her disappointment. What did the woman want from him?

The chopper egg-beat its way back toward the mountain.

"Can I give you a lift?" The director, Lucas Stone, pulled a megaphone away from his lips, motioning for Annie to join him in the helicopter.

Annie glanced at Greg. Casually, deliberately, she twined her arm through his, her sassy smile back in place. "I wanted to dance with the man what brung me."

Greg waved her away. "Go on. That's God talking."

Not so easily shrugged off, Annie kissed him, quick, and ran for the chopper. "I was hoping you'd say that," she shouted over the whirling din. "I love these things!"

The machine whined and lifted off. Greg turned his back on the swirling dust. The view was magnificent. So why was it that all he could remember was her walking at him out of the sun, hair glistening, eyes alight, laughing and dancing, so alive in his arms?

The stunt had almost gone terribly wrong. Thanks to that sticking door, their timing had been off. Or had their kiss gone on too long?

"And which kiss would that be?" he muttered to himself. He spit out a piece of dirt. "How was the take?"

Bill and Jack toed the ground. "He said it was good," Jack replied. *He* meaning Stone.

Greg swung up into the front seat of the Jeep, hiding a wince. They'd brought his battered old Stetson along. He plopped it low over his eyes, unconcerned with how it looked atop the dusty torn tuxedo. "We'll know when we see the rushes."

He'd be interested to see if the printed film showed how real those kisses had been. But it couldn't have caught them lying on the seat, his fingertips on her breast, his tongue in her mouth.

"See you saved your watch," Bill said.

"Always do."

THREE

Annie greeted five members of the stunt crew as she entered the cantina. After checking into the small Western hotel, she'd washed the dust and sweat from her body. It still hummed from the day's excitement. Some things you couldn't wash away. Kisses, for instance. Attraction.

Modestly shrugging off the crew's congratulations on her stunt, she pulled up a chair. "Where's the boss?" she asked.

"Watching the rushes."

"Maybe I'll wander down and see how the shot came out."

"Maybe not," Bill murmured into his beer.

Annie caught Bill and Jack playing angels, innocently examining the beams over the bar. "He doesn't like anyone else seeing the stunt rushes?" she asked.

"He doesn't like dancing on the edge."

Annie could have told them that. "I was so thrilled to see him standing there safe."

A series of mournful clucks and grimly shaking heads told her she was in trouble. "Maybe I'd better go talk to him."

"If he's mad enough, he'll find you."

The rest of the stuntmen put in their two cents' worth.

"Maybe nobody told you, but Greg Ford has no sense of humor."

"Whatsoever."

"Not where stunt work is concerned."

"Ease up, guys, the lady's new around here." Greg's voice rasped behind her like lightly callused fingertips tracing her spine.

She turned. "Hi." Her voice squeaked. The shadow his hat brim cast made her wish she had a Stetson of her own to hide beneath.

"They're giving you a hard time." He dragged out a creaky cane-back chair. Straddling it, he slapped his Stetson on the table. "You did good, Silk. The rushes look fine."

Annie laughed from sheer relief, taking the compliment in stride. "They had me a little worried."

"This beer mine?"

"Been waiting for you, boss."

Greg concentrated on a moisture-dotted bottle. Running his fingers down its sloping neck, he slid it back and forth in tight moist circles on the tabletop.

"Of course, there are a few details we need to discuss about what went on in that car."

Annie's mouth grew dry.

"The door stuck," he added for the others' benefit.

"What happened?" a chorus of male voices asked.

Greg studied them one by one. "It's what *almost* happened. And what you might have said to the director about it." He turned his gaze on Annie.

In the few hours they'd been apart, she'd forgotten the effect those blue eyes had on her.

She mentally ran through the conversation she'd had in the helicopter with the film's director. "He said it looked like we jumped a little late."

Greg nodded, wary as ever. "And?"

Annie shrugged and grinned. "I told him it was *supposed* to look dangerous."

The other men laughed. Even Greg broke down and smiled. He toasted her with the beer bottle. "Thanks."

"Anytime."

"Did he ask about the dance?" Greg's lips barely moved.

The others counted the bubbles in their beer.

Annie lifted her chin. "I told him I love my job."

"It showed."

The others laughed. Greg didn't.

"They got it on film," he added.

He'd sat there in the dark evaluating the stunt, cringing every time they came to the end of the reel. One lone cameraman hadn't gotten the order to cut. He'd filmed a beautiful, gleaming woman in a torn white dress slit halfway up her thigh, throwing herself into Greg's arms on a cliff's edge.

Greg had stood there like a rock.

The man he used to be would have done it, Greg thought, he would've danced. He took a long pull on his warm beer. He hadn't always been so cautious. So tight-assed, he groused silently.

Annie had been absolutely right up there. They were alive. Why not celebrate?

Because living wasn't such a gift when the people you loved were dead. Greg winced and drank again. He recognized self-pity when he tasted it. It tasted like warm beer.

Right now he had a crew to look after, a job to do, and a new member to welcome. There was also the small matter of what really had happened in that car. They hadn't even begun to discuss that.

"So. This is the crew." Greg nodded from left to right. "Bill, you've met. Jack, Antony, Chris, Amos. When we're done trading stories and lying to each other, I'll get you booked in at the hotel."

Annie joined the laughter. "Thanks, but I already am." She tried not to look too cocky. "The stunt went fine. I figured you'd be keeping me on."

The others laughed. Grudgingly, Greg joined them. "Welcome aboard." They shook on it.

She'd pulled her hair into another ponytail; it swished past her cheek when he lifted his beer in a silent offer and she turned him down.

"Bill? Ask the waitress to get the lady a lemonade."

Bill jumped to it.

"Come to think of it, get me one too."

The crew groaned in unison and stood.

"You're no fun at all, boss," Bill said.

"Get lost, all of you," Greg said good-naturedly.

They ambled toward a back room where a poker game was in progress. A companionable silence settled between Annie and Greg. She glanced over, catching the frown furrowing his brow.

Leaning forward, she placed her hand on his arm, too intent on saying what was on her mind to care about the intimacy of the gesture. "Maybe it was my fault. Maybe I didn't hit the door hard enough."

"That explains the *door*," Greg replied, fixing her with a long stare.

Annie's cheeks flushed. She'd never been happier to see a lemonade in her life. The tartness made her mouth water and her lips pucker. So did the waitress's brazen move.

"Hiya," the peroxide blond said to Greg, slinking her thigh against his arm as she set down his lemonade. "Want some extra sugar with that, sugar?"

"Or do you like it tart?" The comment escaped before Annie could stop it. She sensed a flicker of humor in Greg's eyes and sipped her lemonade. Over the rim she glimpsed a group of stuntmen hovering in the door of the poker room, trying to be inconspicuous.

"No, thanks," Greg said to the waitress.

Discouraged, the woman sashayed back to the bar.

Groans and raucous laughter sounded from the back room. Money changed hands. Jack caught Annie's wry glare and gave her a "we tried" shrug.

Boys, Annie thought disgustedly. It was obvious Greg's crew cared about him as much as he cared about them. Maybe they thought a woman was what he needed. Annie surprised herself by agreeing. However, what Greg Ford didn't need was a bottle-blond bimbo in a low-cut Mexican fiesta number. He needed someone who could take him on, shake him up, stand up to him. Someone like Annie Oakley Cartwright.

"Sorry about that, uh—" Greg waved his hand in unconscious imitation of the sway of the waitress's retreating hips. "The guys' idea of a joke. Kind of rude when I'm sitting here with another woman."

"Maybe they think of me as another member of the crew."

He didn't. The flash in his eyes told her so.

Annie desperately tried to drown a frog in her throat. "I should be toasting you with champagne, not lemonade. You saved my life today."

"Maybe it was my mistake that endangered it. I should've had a better idea of what hitting that sidewall would do."

"You can't predict everything."

He shook his head, his eyes fixed on hers. "That's for damn sure."

Her pulse revved and her body felt his weight all over again. "Greg."

"You want to talk about it in here?"

"Not really."

He stood, legs spread on either side of the chair, her gaze momentarily drawn to the glitter of his belt buckle, then up, to the wary turbulence of his eyes. "Let's go," he said.

They walked down a dusty street named High Noon Avenue, part of the hastily constructed Western town. "So, you're checked in," Greg said.

Annie shuddered at memories of their hotel. "Looks like a cross between the Bates Motel and something out of 'Gunsmoke.'"

"Pseudo-authentic."

"But original."

"Oh, completely."

Annie smiled. "I almost expected Miss Kitty to come out and greet me."

"That's her name," he replied in all seriousness. "The lady who manages the place keeps about sixteen flea-bitten furballs in the back."

"Is that what that smell was?"

"Did she put you on the second floor?"

"I told them I was with the stunt crew." She blushed. "I had my fingers crossed at the time."

He gave her an "aw, shucks" tilt of the head and

scuffed the dirt as they walked. "Gotta believe in your-self. Never admit you can fail."

Her heart swelled. "My daddy always said the same thing."

"So what's Rusty up to nowadays?"

"Oh, this and that." Annie was intensely relieved to be talking about a neutral subject. Unfortunately, she had to hedge on this one issue. Her father, a well-known stuntman turned character actor, wouldn't ap-preciate anyone in the industry knowing the condition he was in. "He gets around. He got himself a new van last fall."

"Traveling?"

"You know retired folks. He and my brother Cody were always on the road together."

"And where were you?"

"At home wishing I could get just as dirty and have just as much wind knocked out of me."

"And your mother?"

"She left when I was thirteen. She thought Dad's work was too dangerous, that my hero-worship for him was going to ruin my feminine instincts, that Cody was going to get himself killed—" Annie plunged her fin-gers into the hair at the nape of her neck. "I'm boring you."

"No, you're not."

They walked until she couldn't evade his unspoken question any longer. "Bronco-busting competition, Wichita Falls, three years ago. Cody was thrown. His neck snapped."

Greg shoved his fists in his back pockets. "I thought I'd heard something like that. I was hoping it wasn't a relation."

"It was instantaneous."

"Yeah. Getting over it is what takes forever."

They'd passed the side street with the hotel on it a hundred yards ago. The stars winked overhead, a careless splash of diamonds glistening over the equally uncaring desert.

"So, your Mom disapproved of stunt life," Greg said at last, his voice soft and accommodating, gently and firmly leading her back to a safer subject.

He was good company, Annie thought, intrigued by his sensitivity. "Mom never minded my love of horses. She figured I needed to know about them, living on a ranch. She liked my gymnastics too. Very feminine." Annie laughed with gusto. "She sure hit the ceiling when she found out I'd been sneaking out of ballet class for martial arts lessons though."

"Black belt?"

"Third degree."

He nodded, impressed.

Annie heaved a dramatic sigh. "At last, a man who appreciates me for what I really am! Mom would be so pleased."

Greg chuckled. In the dark it sounded marvelous.

She took a chance and stopped beside him. "Greg, about today."

"It shouldn't have happened."

Annie felt something small and hopeful shrivel inside her.

"In fact, if I'd known about your brother, I'd have never hired you."

"What?" Annie gaped at him. She'd meant to talk about the kiss, not the job. "I can handle the stunts."

"You've got to fall from a bucking horse tomorrow. That's too close for comfort." As if that settled that, he turned to walk away.

Balanced on the balls of both feet, Annie pointed a cocked finger at his retreating back. "Just a minute here! I do gymnastics, trampoline work, two hours of aerobics a day. I run, bike, swim, mountain climb, and rappel. I've been through three courses at the Bob Bondurant High Performance Driving School, and I can handle anything on four hooves, including mules!"

He came to a dead halt six feet away. His narrow hips turned first, then his shoulders. Finally his chin came around, his eyes scanning her. "You calling me a mule?"

Clint Eastwood couldn't have said it better or slower.

Annie gulped. She put her hands on her hips and strode up to him. With her chin atilt, they came nose to nose. "Yes, I am. I can do any stunt work Julie McLean can do."

"Look, Silk, I didn't mean to question your skills. What I meant was, if I'd known you this personally—if I'd *wanted* to know you this personally, I'd have kept you out of anything as unpredictable as a horse stunt. Understand?"

Before she could sputter out an answer, he turned on his boot heel and headed toward the hotel. Annie had two options, try to match him stride for stride and end up walking like Groucho Marx, or jog after him. The hell with pride; she chased him. "That makes no sense, Ford."

"It does to me."

"Then kindly explain it."

In no words or less, he did. He hauled an arm around her waist and clamped her to him. Then he kissed her. Not hard. Not soft. Just kissed her. In the middle of High Noon Avenue.

She felt the resistance coiling inside him; in the way he clutched her arms, holding her yet holding her away; the way he lifted her to her toes instead of bending that stubborn neck of his; the way his determination broke when he moaned the word *Silk*, flattening his hands on her back, tucking her body into his, sliding his hips against her abdomen.

She could tell by the reluctant growl in his throat that he didn't mean to open his mouth, never had. Then she tasted his tongue.

Her heartbeat doubled; her breathing all but stopped. Fireworks went off in her veins and sparklers danced along her skin, warning flares. She twined her arms around his neck.

He set her rudely on her feet. "Does that give you some idea why we can't work together?"

Annie opened her mouth. It stayed that way. "You want me off the picture because you want me?"

"Yep."

"You're going to have to do better than that, Ford."

He leaned toward her.

She literally jumped back. "In complete sentences, if you don't mind."

He staggered back into a slash of moonlight. He scowled at the sky, raking the back of his neck with a half-clenched fist, glaring at all those profligate stars. "Stunt work requires concentration. Getting it on in the backseat of a car—"

"—was the whole idea."

"It got away from us. If we'd been paying more attention, thinking more—"

"Mistakes happen."

"Accidents happen."

"Life happens! Nobody could have predicted whether that door would stick after you rammed the car against the mountain. Nobody."

"If we'd gotten an earlier jump instead of climbing all over each other like a couple of high school kids—"

"Dammit, Greg, we're professionals. We kept our cool and handled it."

"We're supposed to minimize mistakes, not handle them. We create fantasies of danger, not the real thing—"

"The fantasy is thinking you can control everything that comes your way."

"Is it?" He backed her into the shadows, and her shoulder blades bumped the unpainted back of a storefront facade. "You think we can control this?"

Strain outlined the taut planes of his face. Starshine glinted in his narrowed eyes. Only Annie knew how sweetly unraveled her own self-control had become. As any stuntwoman could have told her, "Jump when you know what you're getting into and not a moment before." Greg Ford was more man and more unleashed desire than she'd bargained for. She was in over her head.

He braced an arm against the wall, his palm flat beside her head. In the dark his face hovered near hers. Her cheeks burned. She trembled to think he felt the heat. Like a tumbleweed, her heart skittered away.

"One of us better control this, Silk." With the fingers of his free hand, he captured a strand of hair as it escaped her ponytail. It whispered between his thumb and forefinger. "This work is dangerous enough—"

Annie swallowed. Work, she could handle. "It doesn't have to happen again."

"But it will."

"It won't." She stepped out from under his arm, finding a cooling ray of silvery moonlight in the empty street. "We'll keep our minds on business."

"Will we?"

"You could put a little more effort into it."

"That's what I was about to do."

Annie hoped to high heaven that was a smile in his

voice. The gap between tomboy risks and womanly courage had never seemed so wide. She gathered every scrap she'd ever had and stepped toward him.

He took her offered hand without a word, his grip conforming to hers. A woman could believe in hands like that, strong, sturdy, protective. Annie would have if his lips hadn't told her a dozen darker, more sensual, more dangerous things about the man. She'd warned herself once already today—a careless stuntman could break a leg, a caring one could break her heart. Until she knew a little more about him, until she could handle the explosive combination of their nearness, she'd stick to business.

"All business. Okay, pardner?" She hoped he could see that confident twinkle in her eye. She'd worked damn hard to put it there.

"Okay," he replied reluctantly.

Patting her breastbone, she managed a weak laugh. "I feel like I just got the job."

"Weirdest interview I ever gave."

At last she'd gotten him to laugh. Annie joined in, crooking an arm through Greg's. She gave his hip a bump. "Walk me back to the hotel?"

"You got it."

Their boots thumped on the plank sidewalk, imitation gaslights greeting them as they turned the corner.

"Things might have gone a little smoother if we'd had a chance to talk like this before," Annie said. "We could have laid it all to rest before it even happened."

"You think that would've stopped it?"

"There'd have been fewer false moves."

"Less kissing?"

No kissing at all, Annie thought. Her heart sank. She wasn't a big one for regrets, life was too short. And yet, considering the promises they'd made, this was no time to tell him how thoroughly she'd enjoyed their encounter in the car. She savored it still.

She glanced at Greg out of the corner of her eye. The man needed kissing. He needed teasing and smiles, something to yank him out of that rut he'd placed himself into. She'd agreed that they should keep their distance. So why did she feel she was deserting him?

Because every instinct in her body told her to get right back on if a horse threw her. Even if that horse gently nudged her away. Even if that horse scared her with its barely restrained power. Greg Ford needed somebody in his life—the right kind of somebody. Annie Oakley Cartwright had the idea, hard and small as a seed planted in spring, that she could be that woman.

A tiny voice that sounded mysteriously like the instincts she never doubted, whispered to her. *You could be good for him.*

Another voice, sounding more like her father's common sense said, *Honey, that might be more horse than you can handle.*

One way or the other, she'd have to make up her mind.

❖━━━━━❖

They strode through the swinging doors of the hotel and into the lobby. The narrow room featured a long saloon bar with tables set up opposite it. A jukebox squatted in the corner where a player piano might have stood a hundred years before. Two men circled a pool table. Balls clicked, chalk scraped.

Annie and Greg climbed the creaking wooden stairs to the second floor. She hesitated at the top. Greg resisted steering her left; it would've meant touching her. "Uh, this way."

Miss Kitty had put her right across the hall from him. They paused outside her door.

Annie turned to him, shrugging apologetically. "Movie-set romances—"

"I agree."

"Pitiful."

"Short-term."

"Nothing but complications."

"You got that right."

She stared contritely at her room key. "Well, good night, then."

"'Night."

She closed her door and locked it.

Greg stood in the hallway contemplating her hasty retreat. She'd started the day out like a breath of fresh air. Eight hours around him, and she'd become as cautious and skittish as he was.

Some people would think that funny. Not him. A

hard shot of frustration nagged at him like an old injury on a cold day. He rubbed the back of his neck, wondering why he had that effect on people.

The answer was sitting on the bed when he opened the door to his room, a woman he'd loved for a lot of years, who'd stopped loving him back a long time ago.

He kicked the door closed and picked the photograph up off the bed. He ran his fingers over the silver frame. "Well, Pam, you wouldn't have been too proud of me today."

He lay back, easing a pillow out from under his aching back. Some people talked to plants or cats, he talked to Pam's picture. "I almost got myself and a stuntwoman killed. Miscalculation."

Try as he might, he couldn't keep whipping himself for that one. There wasn't any way in creation he could've predicted that door would stick. Like Annie said, they'd kept their cool and everything worked out. "And if it hadn't?"

He glanced at the photo. "I would've seen you a lot sooner."

It had been five years since her death, and he still couldn't imagine loving anyone else. Assorted aches and pains could be heated or rubbed or ignored. His heart, as far as he was concerned, would never heal. He found it hard to imagine finding another woman like Pam.

Annie Cartwright came to mind unbidden.

"She's ten years younger than me and considerably

prettier. She's blond, willowy, and eighty percent tom-boy."

Pam had been dark and demure, gentle and sweet-natured. She hadn't been sassy or daring. She'd never have provoked him the way Annie Cartwright did at every turn. What they'd had had burned like a glowing ember, a hearth fire. Around Annie Cartwright brush fires erupted, all spark and tinder.

He'd kissed her twice, in a stuffy cramped car, body to body, both of them sweating and breathing hard, and in a moonlit alley, rough and quick and quickly denied.

He could practically hear the lock on her door clicking into place. His urgency had scared her. Hell, it scared him. It had been years since he'd wanted to kiss a woman that way.

Greg chuckled to think what Rusty Cartwright would do if he found out what Greg had been doing with his daughter. And Pam? He glanced at the photo of the laughing brunette and suddenly hurt all over.

"Mr. Ford. We'd like you to come down to the hospital with us." Two policemen had driven out to the Utah Salt Flats. He'd just finished ramming a car into a brick wall to prove that air bags worked. He'd walked away without a scratch. On a street two miles from their home, his wife hadn't been so lucky. The drunk had been going eighty-five at least—

Greg swore and turned over on the creaky bed, setting the photo on the nightstand. "She's blond, okay? Her hair's practically white in some lights."

Pam was always so fragile. So careful. Why didn't she see that guy? Why didn't she swerve, brake, do something?

Greg's voice grated. "Her eyes are blue. Wild-flower blue. Bluebell blue." And she'd probably think he was nuts if she heard him talking like this.

He didn't care. It had kept him together when nothing else had. The people you loved didn't just disappear. He needed to believe that. Love stayed with you, otherwise what was it for?

This last year it had finally dawned on him that these talks had become a way of getting his thoughts in order at the end of the day—nothing more. When he went on location, he packed her picture. He unpacked it. He felt pieces of her slip away.

Restless, he got up and walked into the bathroom, kicking the piles of clothes into some kind of order. He'd showered before viewing the rushes. Wet towels littered the floor. Memories of the stunt cluttered his brain.

He could've sent Jack on the stunt this morning. But Annie had been new, covering up a handful of nerves with a whole lot of cockiness. The minute she'd raised her chin and stuck out her hand to introduce herself, he'd known he had to go with her, to look out for her.

"She handled it real well," he said to the picture as he settled into bed at last. "I think you'd like her."

He turned off the light, refusing to think about how much he liked her.

FOUR

A dream. It had to be. The fact that his eyes were wide open convinced him it wasn't. So did his hammering heart. A ghost would have looked like Pam. The woman standing at the foot of the bed was flesh and blood.

The sudden rush of heat to his groin made him aware of the lingering clamminess on his skin. A grating rasp made his voice brusque. "Annie. What are you doing here?"

She didn't reply.

He ran a hand over his sandpapery chin. The clock said three A.M. Better to curse the darkness than switch on a light guaranteed to slice through his tightly squinted eyes. He yanked the chain anyway.

It had no effect on her glassy stare. "My dress," she said.

"What dress?" Lingering sleep hadn't put that huskiness in his tone. He saw her clearly now.

She wore a tank top, lightly ribbed, nearly see-through. His gaze traveled the shallow valley between her breasts. She wore jockey-style panties, a cotton triangle with narrow strips riding high on her thighs. Her legs were long, her thighs lightly dusted with gold.

Greg cursed and sat up. "You're sleepwalking, aren't you?"

She gazed at the wallpaper ten inches over his head. "Have you seen it? I need it." She began to fret around the room. "I need . . . something to wear . . ." She crossed her arms in front of her and lifted the hem of her tank top.

Greg bolted out of bed. "I get the picture." Naked, he hop-stepped into his boxers.

Annie gazed blankly around her, apparently seeing things he couldn't. He kept his fingers crossed she'd stay that way until he got some clothes on. "Why didn't you tell me you do this?"

No answer. He racked his brain for information about sleepwalkers. His little brother had done it at the age of seven; his dad had dealt with it by hauling the kid over his shoulder fireman-style and depositing him back in the lower bunk.

The image of depositing Annie in his bed, caveman-style, made Greg's mouth go dry. His skin heated at the mere idea of bending that beautiful body over his shoulder, his arm crooked across her bare thighs. He told himself he'd touched her a hundred times that afternoon in the backseat of that car. He could handle it.

Oh no he couldn't.

"I've gotta get you into bed," he muttered. *"Yours."*

His bark made her jump. She veered to the right and opened the closet. "Is it in here?"

"A dress? Hell, probably."

Holding her elbow, he gingerly led her across the room, keeping the rest of his body a good three feet from hers. He reached for the knob, about to edge backward into the brightly lit hall. He paused. What if Miss Kitty or a crew member saw them cavorting across the hall in their skivvies? And what would putting her in her room accomplish? Nothing could stop her from unlocking her door and coming out again. The next time she might not run into someone so obliging.

He closed the door to his room. She stood there in the harsh light looking confused, anxious, as if she might wake up any moment. He turned off the light. Moonlight touched her legs.

"I need—" she said.

"Shh."

If she wasn't a ghost, maybe she'd been sent by one. He smiled wryly at the idea Pam was punishing him for all his dirty thoughts. He wouldn't be surprised if it turned out this whole thing was a dream. *Or a gift* . . .

"Get in bed," he said, steering her toward it, his exasperated whisper tinged with shame, regret, frustration. He'd never thought himself capable of what he was about to do. The idea made his jaw clench.

"I—"

"Get in bed." Hell, if she was going to walk right in, dressed like that—

Her body yielded by degrees. Her breasts, pert and conical, flattened subtly as she lay back. He watched her snuggle into the pillow, stretch her long legs, finding the places warmed by him.

Greg swallowed a knot the size of a walnut. "That's good." His voice was as hoarse as the old blanket was scratchy. He left it folded at the foot of the bed. He lifted the edge of the sheet, drawing it up her body, trailing one finger's callused tip the length of her leg, skimming golden stubble, an intimate revelation. Not for the first time that day he wondered what kind of man he'd become.

He touched her again.

"He isn't that kind of man."

Annie strode toward the corral on the edge of the set. Her legs quaked, as tottery as a newborn colt's. She wasn't completely sure what had happened the night before, but she had a good idea. She'd woken up in Greg Ford's bed. Her body still tingled at the very idea of it. She'd smelled his leather and spice aftershave on the pillowcase. She'd seen his clothes on the floor.

She saw the cot he'd slept on blocking the door.

And a picture of a smiling brunette.

"It happened," she said to herself. "Whatever it was. We deal with it."

She caught sight of him two hundred yards ahead and knew that would be easier said than done. The yoke of his broad shoulders widened as he rested his arms on the top rail of the corral. Tight jeans worn grey in spots, torn in others, encased his narrow hips. She knew from experience how firm and corded the legs inside those jeans were. Was it a memory from the car stunt or the previous night?

"In your dreams, Cartwright."

And if it hadn't been a dream?

Blood pounded in her ears like a herd of stampeding bison. Her body ached in a lot of places. Muscles felt stretched, sore; a string of faint bruises shadowed her thigh.

"Yesterday's fall," she insisted.

Or last night's.

"Nothing happened." She gestured for emphasis.

A member of the dolly crew looked up. Annie grinned tightly as she passed. Fortunately, a woman rehearsing her lines wasn't that unusual on a movie set. Except she intended these lines exclusively for Greg Ford.

He turned as if he'd sensed her coming, each rigid inch of him. A dusty black cowboy hat slanted low on his forehead, shading his eyes. "Mornin'."

Annie came up beside him at the railing, every practiced word drying up in her throat. "Morning," she croaked.

He gnawed a piece of straw clamped between his lips. Together they stared straight ahead. A trainer led a black horse around the ring on a rope. Annie peered at Greg out of the corner of her eye. Except for the steady beat of a vein in his cheek, he didn't move a muscle.

The horse grunted. The horse tossed its head and bared its teeth. Greg Ford stood like a stone.

"Is that Dickens?" Annie asked.

"Yep. He's a handful."

She caught the hint. He didn't want her doing this stunt. Annie almost sighed with relief; she'd tackle the easy issues first. In fact, she'd leap on them like a dieting starlet on a bucket of fried chicken.

Balancing her behind on the top rail, Annie motioned the horse nearer, stroking its neck. The trainer handed her the rope and stepped away. Annie murmured sweet nothings to the apprehensive animal. "Aw, I can ride him just fine," she purred in the horse's ear. "Can't I, Dickens?"

Greg pulled the brittle straw out of his mouth, snapping it between his thumb and forefinger. He reached for another sticking out of a hay bale. "You think so?"

The ritual of soothing the horse had soothed some of Annie's fears. Tension, coiled in her stomach like an unused lasso, dissipated for the first time this morning. She turned to Greg, smiling easily. "You never really know a horse until you're on it."

He raised his gaze from the juncture of her thighs. "No, you don't."

The lasso became a fuse he lit. The fire sizzled all the way to her toes. "What I meant—"

The fresh piece of straw shifted from one corner of his mouth to the other. "Yeah?"

"I can handle this."

"Which *this* do you mean?"

Annie hopped down off the rail, slapping the backs of her jeans with her palms. Greg scanned the horizon, the rings beneath his eyes a dusky purple, the wrinkles etched beside his eyes as deep as dry arroyos.

"I didn't know," she said earnestly. "If I had, last night would have never happened."

"Know what?"

"That you were married."

It took him a minute. "Pam's picture," he said.

"I would have never done that—I mean, I would have never done that anyway, not if I was awake—I certainly wouldn't have gone to your room if I knew you were married. Awake or asleep." She took a deep breath. It hadn't been the greatest speech, but she'd said it. However, one nagging question remained. What had happened in his bed?

She could always come right out and ask, she thought.

When pterodactyls fly.

Annie found her own piece of straw and nervously nibbled. "It was a sign I trusted you," she said. "Sleepwalkers never purposely endanger themselves."

"And what do you consider dangerous?"

His derisive smile made her knees weak. She

couldn't believe he would have taken advantage of her in such a situation. She wouldn't believe it.

A horn sounded from the set. As if on cue a half dozen crew members who'd tactfully kept their distance converged on Greg seeking instructions, relaying information. The second-unit cameras were in place, the dollies set, the charges planted. Eventually the crowd cleared and Annie had Greg to herself again.

The interruptions had given her time to think. He was being uncooperative and distant, like a man ashamed of what he'd done. But that cot. Would a man who'd taken advantage of the situation have chosen such a chaste sleeping place?

"We have to get moving on the horse stunt," he said, striding toward the barn. "We can talk later."

Annie followed him. "Will you accept my apology?"

He turned, glancing down at the spot where she gripped his arm. That look could stop a lot of men in their tracks. She refused to let go.

"What exactly are you apologizing for?"

He knew darn well she couldn't remember. She quivered inside at his low mocking tone. "You tell me."

He had to admire her courage. He'd half expected her to be packed and on her way back to L.A. when she found herself in his room this morning. He'd been down at the corral since six A.M. wondering how to replace her—and why he was so eager to. "You don't know?"

She shook her head, her eyes vulnerable but unwavering. Such strength in such a small frame, he thought, and ninety percent of it coming from the inside. But for all her boldness, there were fragile places in Annie Cartwright, parts a man wanted to protect. Even if it meant protecting her from himself.

She'd scared the daylights out of him last night, reigniting desire he'd thought dead long ago. It hit him like a runaway train, like lightning striking, like a woman throwing herself in his arms on a cliff.

She waited for answers he didn't have. He needed to get his bearings, sexual and otherwise. To do that, he needed to back her off. "A woman who sleepwalks into a man's room at that hour of the night can expect just about anything."

She swallowed.

He knew what that tasted like. "Do you do that often?"

"Once in a blue moon."

He remembered her body by moonlight, silver and gold.

"Talking to you about Cody and Dad must have got me thinking about too many things," she said, "disturbed my sleep." Judging from her eyes, it bothered her still.

Greg squinted at the crew members edging nearer. As if a laser had drawn a line in the sand, they kept their distance. He hooked his thumbs in the back of his waistband, dug a heel in the dirt, and raised the steel toe of his cowboy boot. "Maybe wrestling around in the car did it. Or kissing me. Maybe you came back for more."

"Maybe the close call on the stunt scared me more than I realized."

"Or the closer call behind the hotel?"

"It doesn't have to be sexual." She lowered her voice. "On rare occasions I sleepwalk. That's all. Something wouldn't let me rest—"

"—until you came to my room." He angled his body in toward hers, blotting out the morning sun. He watched the way she stood her ground, the way her eyes darkened in his shadow and her cheeks flushed. "You rested fine then. You lay right down."

Her heart hammered. A chill spiraled down her back. "I didn't know you were a married man."

"I'm not."

"Involved, then."

For a second he took pity on her. He wasn't so gentle with his own emotions. "My wife died five years ago."

Annie felt as if a fist had landed smack in her solar plexus, like a bad fall in karate class. "I'm sorry."

"A car accident. It was instantaneous."

It's the getting over it that takes forever. Annie remembered the phrase as clearly as if he'd spoken it aloud. She watched him seek the horizon again. The sky behind him seemed to go on forever, blue and empty. She wanted to touch him, to help.

"It's been a long time," he said.

Not judging by the pain in his eyes. She knew he'd

reject any sympathy she offered; the way he held himself kept her at a distance. Nitwit, who are you protecting? she thought suddenly. She stepped forward and put her arms around his waist.

"Hey!"

She squeezed until she couldn't squeeze anymore. A teardrop stained his denim shirt. "Why didn't you tell me? No, don't say it. That's just you, isn't it?"

It made sense now. Every one of the other stuntmen knew about this—that's why they were so protective of their gruff boss. That's why a rugged, handsome, sexy man needed friends fixing him up with women he turned down.

Standing stiff in her arms, he hesitated. Then he touched her hair. "Annie, it's okay."

A few minutes earlier, she'd been ready to call a halt to every bit of sexual awareness sparking between them. Now she knew the reason he'd dug himself such a deep hole. He needed her more than ever.

She blinked away sentimental tears and flashed him a dazzling smile, giving him a good hard squeeze before letting go. "I'm going to give you the splashiest horse stunt you've ever seen. Okay, boss?"

A production assistant in a baseball cap bustled in, ignoring their tender moment. "Ready to go, Ford?"

Greg never took his eyes from hers. "Just about."

" 'Just about' don't fry the bac—"

"Yeah."

"Yeah?"

"Yeah."

The assistant spoke into his walkie-talkie. "He says they're ready."

A handful of static answered him. The assistant cleared his throat. "He wants it wrapped by noon; think you can do that?"

"We can."

Annie watched the man trot away. It was already seven-thirty A.M., late by movie-set standards. Judging from the time Greg had spent walking her through the car stunt, she'd been sure he'd take even more time re-creating the stunt that had injured Julie McLean. "We can have this done by noon?" she asked.

"We've gone over it twice already." A guilty look darkened his face; his gaze slid to the barn door.

A stuntman in a long narrow skirt and silk blouse stood in the shadows, trying to get his ladylike boot heel in the stirrups of Dickens's saddle. Sidestepping, the horse foiled him every time.

"Hold on just a minute!" Annie shouted at Greg's retreating back as he stalked toward the wooden structure.

"Shh," he commanded, "you'll scare the horse."

"Horsefeathers," she hissed, confining her argument to urgent whispers. "You aren't sending a stuntman in a wig on *my* stunt."

"That's what I planned."

"Since when?"

"Since last night." He held up a palm. "Since we agreed this was business."

"But this *is* my business!"

"And coordinating stunts is mine. After what you told me about your brother dying in a fall, I'm not putting you on anything that bucks or bolts."

"Does that mean nothing happened in your bed?" The minute she said it, every nerve in Annie's body went on alert.

Greg came to a dead halt, then turned. "Did you want it to?"

Horses stamped in their stalls. Dickens's hooves tapped as he evaded Tony's repeated attempts to mount him.

Annie took a shallow breath. "I need to know."

Greg squinted at the barn's dark interior. Seeing how reluctant he was to say it, Annie wasn't sure she wanted to hear it. She knew from direct personal experience that Greg Ford had more man in him than she was ready to handle. She could have sworn he had a streak of honor and integrity to go with it.

But every man had his limits. She'd brought him to the edge of his more than once. Maybe last night he'd crossed that line.

A string of Spanish curses broke their silence. Tony clutched the knee Dickens had kicked. The horse lashed out again. Tony tore off his wig and threw it in a pile of straw. "I will not ride this horse!"

"Whoa," Annie said, rushing to the horse's side. The air seemed thinner, easier to breathe, none of that oven-hot breathless sensation she felt standing beside Greg. "Whoa, baby. Calm down."

The horse whinnied and nipped at her hand. She

deftly stepped aside and continued stroking his neck. "It'll be fine. That *attractive* young man in the skirt won't ride you, I promise."

Tony's dark eyes flashed while he told her what he thought of the horse's lineage in graphic, albeit Spanish, terms. Annie chuckled and continued stroking, getting Dickens to temporarily tolerate her presence.

Greg sauntered up beside them. She half expected holsters on his hips and spurs jingling when he walked. "Tony's gone over the route," he said. "He knows the stunt."

"It's too late to get anyone else, and Tony just refused to do it. Although he does look very fetching in a dress." She batted her lashes at the young stuntman.

Tony flushed and looked away, only to be met by the grins and catcalls of five stuntmen outside lining the railings of the corral. "Come on out, Tony, honey," they hooted, whistling their appreciation.

Like a matador with a red cape, Tony whipped off the wraparound skirt and flung it to the ground. Annie picked it up. She found the short slit along the side, blithely ripped it eight inches more to give herself some legroom, then slipped the skirt around her waist. Ducking behind Dickens, she reached up under it to wriggle out of her jeans. Her white blouse doubled for the one Costumes gave Tony.

She emerged from behind her four-legged dressing room and twirled in place. "Dressed and ready to go, boss."

The stunt crew applauded. "More leg!"

She lowered her voice. This was strictly between her and Greg. "This is what I came for. Let me show you what I can do."

She knew her words were loaded with double meaning. Apparently he'd rather crack into a hundred rock-size pieces than acknowledge whatever had happened the night before. Fine. She'd pretend nothing had happened.

With one light hop, she put her foot in the stirrup and swung her leg over the saddle. "Ready when you are, boss."

Greg scowled. He couldn't very well drag her off the horse and he knew it. "Tony will walk you through the routine."

"Where'll you be?"

"Watching." He spat the word out like so much dust, then took Dickens's bridle and led them into the sunlight.

Sensing his audience, Dickens danced. So did Annie's nerves. She bent over the horse's neck, promising him one heckuva workout when this was over.

Her eye caught Greg's. A private smile curved his lip. "You talking to me or the horse?"

Color raced to her cheeks. "The horse."

"Good."

She'd been born so fair, every emotion glowed pink in her cheeks. Fortunately, she'd always found the nerve to face up to her emotions. Sometimes that nerve was harder to find than others. She dredged up a smile and more confidence than she felt. "The game is up,

Ford. You won't tell me what happened last night because you want to scare me off this picture. Well, I'm not buying. You took me in. You put me to bed. You dug out that cot and slept on it."

"Who says I slept?"

The circles under his eyes testified to that. She raised her chin. Dickens sensed it, tossing his mane in imitation. Annie retrieved the reins from Greg. "Unless you tell me otherwise, I'm assuming you were a perfect gentleman."

"Nobody ever accused me of being that. Especially women." Greg stepped in close, his back to the onlooking crew, his head even with her saddle. He glanced at the way her legs spread, the skirt softly sagging. He noticed how tightly she wound the reins around one hand. "Nervous?"

"Not around horses."

"You like to ride; it shows." His gaze slipped from her face to her hips. "You have a good seat."

She unconsciously tightened her thighs. Dickens responded. It took her a second to quiet him down. Turning him in a tight circle, Annie brought him back around to Greg and that subtle knowing smile that was beginning to irritate her no end. "Ready to get this show on the road?"

He stopped her with an unexpected question. "When you woke up this morning and saw where you were, were you surprised?"

"Of course."

"Happy?"

A strange and disturbing exhilaration had followed her around all morning. It didn't mix well with the potential humiliation of her situation. "Surprised," she stated.

"So you rushed right down here."

"I was late."

He curled his hand around her ankle, his touch squeaking against the polished leather of her boot. He didn't touch the expanse of leg bared by her slit skirt. He didn't have to. "I don't suppose you had time to shave your legs."

Before she could answer, he'd turned and walked away.

They walked through it three times. Trotted through it twice. They fired a few charges to see how skittish the horse was. Greg stood behind the rail, barking orders but otherwise leaving Annie in Tony's care.

Any more self-control and the man would bust, she thought. He hovered, he hounded, he second-guessed every twist and turn of the ten-second, hundred-yard, one-take stunt. The guilt about Julie's injury weighed on him like a fifty-pound saddle slung across a shoulder. Despite their run-in this morning, he was determined to keep her safe. It was costing him. If he popped another Tums, she'd buy stock in the company.

But that was as far as her sympathy stretched.

Thanks to his shaving remark, she sat her horse like Lady Godiva, stripped and naked in his imagination and her own. Every time he walked near enough to the horse to reach out, she pulled her ankle in closer.

Every time, the horse responded, skittering to the side.

"Concentrate," Greg yelled.

"I'm trying."

"If you can't do this, for any reason, you tell me now."

She pulled Dickens up short and aimed him toward the starting line. "We're going back to the beginning. Maybe that's a good idea for all of us!"

The crew had planted a gauntlet of yellow flags to indicate where the charges were placed. After Annie memorized their location, they'd be pulled up. She'd race the horse into the corral, circle the ring, then jump the breakaway rail at the end while sand and dirt exploded around them in imitation gunfire. When they cleared the last jump, she was to slouch in her saddle as if shot, then slip out of the saddle and fall to the ground. Simple enough.

It'd be half past ten by the time they were ready to film. It'd be half past forever by the time Annie's heart stopped zinging in her chest. She felt Greg's hand still curved around her ankle as if he'd clamped a vice around it. She felt light fingers tracing fine blond hairs on her leg.

Dickens tensed when she did.

"Concentrate!" Greg yelled. "You would've walked right into a blasting cap."

"Ford," the assistant whined.

Greg shot him a glance. The little man shut up. "We practice it again or she doesn't do it."

Annie silently thanked him. All morning he'd steadfastly refused to let anyone rush her. The production assistant was on his back. Greg was on her case. Her nerves were rubbed raw. If only she'd stop clenching her thighs, urging the horse in ways he wasn't supposed to be urged. She made the mistake of glancing at Greg as they trotted by the rail. Speaking of uncontrollable urges . . .

"Concentrate!"

Damn.

She brought Dickens to a halt in front of Greg. "It'd be easier just to go through with it."

"Would it?"

The subtle thread of frustration in his reply made her envision a dozen more sensual possibilities. "He wants to run, I say let him."

To her surprise, Greg agreed. Clutching his stopwatch, he took his place beside the camera. He put on a headset, communicating with the cameras, Special Effects, and the rest of the crew. Annie trotted Dickens toward the edge of town to await her signal.

She ran through a relaxation exercise, collecting her nerves the way she gathered the reins. Concentration was paramount. "All right, Dickens, time to impress the boss."

FIVE

She screwed up. They'd barely galloped into the corral when a blast sent Dickens shying so hard right, Annie had to grab the saddle horn to stay on. She bit back disappointment, blaming herself for the aborted stunt in language harsher than any Greg Ford might use. From the look on his face as he approached, he was about to try.

"Are you okay?" he asked.

"Fine. I'm sor—"

"And the horse?"

Her apology froze in her throat. "He isn't spooked."

The harshness in his eyes softened briefly. "Let's try it again." For a moment she wondered whether he meant them or the stunt.

He walked back to the camera, the production

assistant trailing him like a cocker spaniel who'd seen a leash.

"You said noon," the little man squawked.

"I lied."

Annie chuckled. Whatever kind of man he was, he genuinely believed the safety of his crew came before budgets and timetables. He'd probably be surprised to know how much she admired him for that.

Jumping Dickens over some rails to keep his attention focused while the crew reset the charges, Annie wiped a hand across her forehead, baking in the late morning sun. No sooner had she finished than Bill came around the corner of the barn, hat in hand.

"Greg said to put this on while you wait. It'll be another fifteen minutes."

She yanked the Stetson low on her forehead in imitation of its donor and rode to the edge of the set. Warmth spread through her at his consideration. A ticklish sensation curled down her back at the idea he'd been watching her. She imagined how he must have watched her while she slept. The warmth turned to slow baking heat. "It's just a hat," she muttered. "He'd do the same for any crew member."

In return, she ought to do something for him. Show off her strengths, erase any mistaken impression he had about her. Nailing this stunt would be a nice place to start. She could even improve on it. She got an idea.

A horn blared on the set.

In a matter of seconds, life sorted itself into thinking or doing. Time became elastic, the moment stretched. Risk had a way of condensing life into moments of pure concentration, intense living. Annie loved the sensation.

Trusting her mount, her instincts, and her skill, she urged the horse forward in a burst of speed, intuiting every move Dickens made, evading explosions of sand with dash and style.

She aimed him at the final rail. They jumped. When they landed, Annie made sure his feet were under him before she pulled the reins down and to the side. Like a well-practiced show pony, he went down neighing. She somersaulted off, rolling as if thrown by a powerful force.

Annie heard the order to cut and lifted her head. The horse lay panting on his side. "Stop milking it, Dickens, the stunt's over." The horse scrambled to his feet. His trainer ran up and caught the reins.

Annie let her head fall back, exhausted as much by the nerve-straining wait as the actual fall. Her body thrummed like a live wire. Gosh, she loved this job. The tomboy in her wanted to climb a tree and hang monkey-style from the branches, yelling "Yahoo."

The pounding of running feet vibrated against the back of her head. Slate blue eyes in a tanned and weathered face appeared over her. "What's wrong? Don't move."

The hoarse bark of concern left something to be desired. "Never go into medicine, Greg, you have a terrible bedside manner."

"Don't move!"

"I'm fine. See?" She wiggled her toes inside her boots and did the same with her fingers. She sat up, shaking dirt out of her hair. Beaming, she gave him a peck on the cheek. "I thought you'd be impressed. I took that extra fall because—"

Still talking, she scampered to her feet, slapping dust off her skirt. Silence yawned around her. She'd been so busy scratching the grit off her scalp, she'd missed the scowl darkening Greg's face. The loose ring of stuntmen grew as still as the Petrified Forest.

"You what?!" Greg erupted.

"I wanted to make it look good."

What began as a nonchalant admission escalated to a shouting match in front of the entire crew.

"It looked like you broke your beautiful stubborn neck!"

"It was supposed to!"

"We didn't practice it."

"We didn't have to. I know how to take a fall."

"Or a tumble?"

Her eyes flared. If he was going to hint at what had happened the previous night in front of all these people, he'd have one hell of a fight on his hands. "Don't you dare talk to me like that."

"You're the one who doesn't dare. Not on my set. You do what we planned and not one twist more. Improvising is *not* allowed."

"But it looked more dangerous that way."

"It *is* more dangerous," he bellowed. "That's exactly why you don't do it!" He stalked toward the barn. "Report! Now!"

Annie was furious enough to follow him.

Bill twirled her hat brim clockwise in his hands before inching forward to hand it to her. "I don't think this'll help, but . . ."

Annie seized the hat. "Thanks."

"Remember what happened to Jackson for hotdogging?"

"But I wasn't—" She caught herself short. Hotdogging was exactly what she'd done. "But I only wanted—" Shoulders sagged. "He's going to have my head on a platter, isn't he?"

"Or else he's going to chew out another part of your anatomy."

Bill swatted Chris with his Stetson. "Shush."

They all squinted at the gaping barn door. Brilliant desert sunshine made the threshold as dark as Hades.

"Making him wait isn't going to make it better," Bill said.

Annie sashayed toward the barn, pretending more nerve than she felt. She threw the crew one last glance. "Go ahead and appreciate, boys. This may be the best move I've made all day."

It might just be her last.

The stable was new, looked a hundred years old, and smelled the way stables always smelled. It housed

ten horses. Annie listened to their huffing and shuf-
fling, inhaling the sharp aroma of hay.

"I don't know what it is," she announced, planting
her feet in the doorway, "but the smell of manure
always makes me feel right at home."

Standing with his shoulder against a stall, Greg
cracked a snide smile.

"That's one of my daddy's lines," she said. "You
could laugh a little."

"Did Rusty take crazy risks like that?"

"Worse." She wiped some dust off her torn blouse.
The fall had torn it nearly to the point of indecency,
exposing a flash of black lace.

"I fire hot dogs," Greg stated.

Roast them was more like it, she thought.

"Anybody dumb enough or reckless enough to risk
his life to impress me isn't going to be on my crew
long."

Why was it she could find herself standing on thin
ice in the middle of a desert? Annie kept the sassy
comeback to herself. She cleared her throat and swept
back a handful of hair. A couple of twigs stuck out like
antennae, picking up trouble, danger, and more sexual
static. She shook it out, her hair swishing across her
back.

Greg remembered the exact moment she'd lost the
ribbon that tied it back. She'd gone down in a heap, a
shower of ivory hair sweeping the sky. Greg remembered her small body hitting the ground, the thud that

hit him like a fist, the shot of fear as he waited for her to move.

On one level, he knew a clean fall when he saw one. That didn't mean he trusted fate. Once upon a time, he'd dared to. It had laughed in his face. "You're suspended indefinitely."

"Do I get to say anything in my defense?"

"You don't have one."

"You haven't given me a chance."

"Give? It's a chance I can't *take*. After that sleep-walking incident I should have scrubbed you from the stunt. That's got to affect your work."

"Only if you want me doing stunts in my sleep," she snapped.

"How do you know that isn't exactly what you did?"

She returned his unflinching stare. Her knees quaked. "Nothing happened."

"You could've been raped."

"I could've fallen down the stairs, lit a fire, or walked out into traffic. I didn't do any of it."

"How do you know?"

"I know my body."

"Then you know you have a mole beside your navel. Dark brown, not black, Annie."

Her tongue felt like lead. Tasted like it too. She felt as if she'd inhaled the shaft of sunlight piercing one of the windows. The barn was musty and stuffy. Light hovered so thick with dust motes, she could have reached up and snagged a handful of it. She couldn't tear her eyes from Greg's. *His* warmth lit intimate corners of her soul, making her acutely aware of every inch he might have examined. His gaze never wavered.

Hers did. "You looked," she said, crossing her arms.

"That's not all I could have done."

"You didn't."

"True. I watched." The anger in his voice subsided to a tired rasp.

She shrugged, acutely aware of the weight of her blouse sliding over her shoulders, the breath of air slipping inside, skimming her breast. "Is that all?"

"It was enough." He stalked toward her, hands clenched at his sides. "I watched you breathe. I watched you lie in my bed while the light touched your body, touched it in places I didn't dare. You think I *slept* on that cot?"

"I'm sure I don't want to know."

He'd curled on it, tossed on it. He'd been a dad-blamed white knight and had paid the price for it right up until dawn. "My body still aches. It's called incompletion, Annie."

His eyes studied her scathingly from head to toe, from her lips, luscious and pale, to the patches of fire on her cheeks, to smudges of dirt like a dusting of amber powder. "I damn near memorized every inch of you last night, from the way your panties ride up to the way your tank top lifted when you put your arm up to cradle your head."

"How poetic," she said, an unwelcome flutter in her voice.

"I wanted you to cradle *me*, to part your legs and hold me between them, the two of us in the moonlight, me sliding into you."

Her head came up.

He wouldn't let her back away, holding her with no more than his words. "I figured if I got in bed, you'd struggle. Maybe. For a minute. All I'd have to do is kiss you and you'd want it as badly as I wanted it."

"Dream on."

"I did, wide awake and dreaming, Annie, this close to doing something no decent man would even consider." He turned away. "Hell, you probably would have screamed."

She could barely swallow. A band of sweat glistened on his forehead. A droplet trickled between her breasts. He'd nicked his cheek in two places; after a night of pent-up frustration he'd tried to shave. She hadn't.

"And my legs?" she asked, her voice nearly gone, her nerves spent. "How did you know—"

"I touched them when I put you in bed."

She waited him out. He refused to elaborate. She hadn't learned anything she hadn't already guessed. Yet somehow, instead of defusing the situation, his confession made it worse. More intimate. Infinitely more erotic. "You didn't have to tell me all this."

"You were there. You should know what you almost got yourself into."

She trembled all over. It wasn't fear. It started deep inside and shimmered along her skin like a cool flame, like the heavy tactile air. "I'm sorry. Some part of me must have trusted you."

"Silk?"

Her heart tripped at the whispered sound of her nickname, the severity in his eyes as he turned back to her. "Yes?"

"Trusting me was your first mistake."

He hauled her against him. His mouth came down on hers. He let her back them into an empty stall, but he didn't let her go. Stars danced in the motes of dust scared up by their tangled feet. Her back came up against a wall of wooden slats.

She opened her mouth to argue. His tongue filled it. She raised her head to defy him. His hands held it there, plundering her mouth with fervent thrusts. She shoved the flat of her hands against him. The hard nubs of his nipples pressed against her palms, glorying in her touch.

Finally he reared back, panting. His hips pressed against her, sending shock waves through her. "You came to me because some part of you wanted this. All of you wants it, Annie."

"No." The word sounded weak. She hadn't wanted this last night, hadn't deliberately gone to his room. But here and now, swept up in his embrace, she couldn't deny him.

The voice she heard was a woman's, but it couldn't be hers. It moaned when he opened her mouth for another kiss, groaned when he clamped his hand on the small of her back and urged her against him. The body she thought she knew molded to him, melting, welcoming.

Making love with him would be honest, blunt, one amazing roller coaster ride. The emotional risks merged with the physical excitement. A pure surge of living shook her to her core.

She'd sensed passion in him, courage, caring, plus the strength needed to bottle it all up so tightly, the passion never broke free. In her arms he strained to the breaking point like a wild horse on the prairie, corralled, caught. Like Dickens leaping over the last rail. Annie wanted to be riding him when the explosion came.

His hand trespassed between them. He filled his palm with her breast, his thumb scraping across her nipple.

"Greg." It was getting away from her. The sensations overwhelming her sense. Logic dissolved into pure sensuality. She felt the well of loneliness surrounding him—the real need. She felt the rake of his teeth against her throat, his harsh breathing against her ear. Anger was mixed up in it as much as loss or fear. He was punishing her for that fall, for making his heart lurch, for making it react at all, punishing her for the torture she'd put him through the previous night.

This wasn't the time or place, Annie thought, dimly hearing a Jeep drive by outside. It sure as hell wasn't any way for him to win an argument. Her fingers curled through his hair, mussing it, gripping it. "Stop," she panted.

"Stop." She tugged on his earlobe.

He ignored her. Another bite, another moan.

She gave his ear a sharp yank.

He cursed and jumped back. She planted her heels and shoved him for all she was worth. He moved one step. She glared at him in the swirling light. "You stop when I say stop."

He counted to three, sizing up her obstinate pose. He took her chin in his hand. "And what do I do when you come to my bed? You wanted that kiss, Annie, and every other one we've had."

"Since I don't make a habit of kissing men I don't want to kiss, you're absolutely right. But get this, Mister Ford, I'm not some sex-starved starlet looking for a roll in all this hay!"

"No?"

"Never."

"You got a problem with me, say it."

"You're closed up tighter than Fort Knox. You should live a little, enjoy."

He gave a husky laugh, chafing his lips with his hand. "I *was* enjoying." He stepped toward her.

She crossed her arms in a universal signal for "Not interested, buster." Greg stopped, too stubborn to move aside. Annie tried to step around him. He waited a beat, then let her.

Annie marched into the aisle. "What I was trying to say was, you need a woman."

"Are you offering?"

"I meant a real one."

"That body didn't feel fake to me."

"Don't be crude."

"I got the feeling you liked crude."

"On occasion."

She congratulated herself for that surprised look in his eyes. He'd been trying so hard to frighten her, to scare her away with a display of raw need. Playing rough might frighten a daintier woman, but not Annie Cartwright. The dare excited her more than she wanted to admit. "You need more than a sex partner."

A bemused smile crooked his mouth. "Matchmaking so soon?"

"Women are more than sex objects to you, no matter how much you pretend otherwise."

Stepping forward, he shrewdly took advantage of the fact she was too stubborn to back down too. "You know damn well we weren't pretending."

"You could have your pick of women and you know it."

"Maybe I don't want them."

She touched her swollen lips. "That didn't feel like not wanting to me."

"Then what'd you stop me for?"

"You need someone you can't push around."

"And God appointed you."

"Yeah." Hands on her hips, fanny jutting out and chin jutting forward, Annie got in his face. "I won't coddle you, nurse you, or baby you. I'll be honest with you, argue with you, and grab you by the short hairs if I have to, anything to make you notice all the life you've been missing. Take a risk on a relationship. One-night stands are for cowards."

She lit up like a rocket when she got on a roll, Greg thought. Her eyes glistened and her face flushed. "I'm turning into a hard, bitter man, and you're the woman to cure me." He'd meant it as a tease. It came out like the truth.

It surprised him to his soul to see his hand reach out, his thumb brushing a spot of dust off her cheekbone. The sounds outside, the smells inside, faded. All that mattered was how blue her eyes were, how wide the pupils became when he lowered his mouth to hers. Their lips brushed and touched. He kissed the woman who just might cure him.

She didn't answer. He skimmed the backs of his fingers over her breast. If he hadn't felt her quiver, he would have read it in her eyes. Her nipples remained erect, sensitive, and tender. Kind of how he felt. He smiled. "This is what I've been missing, Annie. This. Long, slow, and deep. Rough, fast, and wild." Staying alive was one thing. He'd nearly forgotten what it meant to *be* alive. "You want to show me what I've been missing? You've got a deal."

She threw her arms around him. "Then reinstate me."

"What?" He'd expected hesitations, conditions, not open-armed, openhearted acceptance.

"We'll dance on the edge; heck, we'll tango. I'll do an even better stunt next time."

He stiffened, the image of her hitting the ground too vivid. "No way. You took a risk we didn't rehearse."

"Nothing went wrong."

"It could have."

"It didn't."

"It could have."

She threw up her hands. "You sound as if you're talking about last night!"

"Last night I was this close to crawling into bed with you—"

"So you like to think. If you'd tried anything, I would have woken up and—"

"And what?" He yanked her toward him. Her chest bumped his.

"This," she declared. She planted her back foot, threw her other leg across his and, with one well-practiced twist, sent him sprawling on his back on the dirt floor.

A piece of straw pricked his neck. Pigeons hooted and cooed in the loft above. Something wet and white landed on his chest with a plop.

Annie clamped a hand over her mouth, unsuccessfully smothering a guffaw. "Point taken?"

Greg sat up scowling, his arms balanced on his knees. He grudgingly thrust out his hand. "Taken."

Annie bowed magnanimously and offered him a lift up.

The moment she planted her heels for leverage, she

realized her mistake. A split second later Greg stood over her, brushing off his hands and warmly smiling down. "You're not the only one who knows judo, Silk."

Lying flat on her back while he hovered over her wasn't such a wise idea, considering the wild-ride kiss they'd shared moments earlier. The same memory seemed to occur to him, turning the twinkle in his eyes to a glowing ember.

"I could have overpowered you any time last night," he stated, voice hoarse and low. "Say uncle."

He would have to choose a phrase guaranteed to get her dander up. She bit her lip. She *hated* to lose. "You're right," she said. "I won't do it again."

He didn't ask whether she meant coming to his room or hotdogging on stunts. Maybe he thought she'd given up on everything.

Stubborn mule, she thought. She batted her lashes. "Help me up?"

He extended his hand.

It was so easy, she was almost ashamed. Her yank bent him forward. Her boot heel connected with his abdomen. A straight-leg kick lifted him and sent him flying over her head.

The top of his head resting against the top of her head, they watched the pigeons flit through the rafters.

"Somebody could get hurt doing this," Greg grumbled.

"I don't respond well to dares."

"You know, there's a reason we choreograph fight scenes. One wrong move—"

Annie let out such a snort of pure frustration, one of the horses turned to see. She twisted onto her side and wriggled around to face him, startled to find he'd done the same. His lips were inches away. His breath fluttered on her face. She inhaled, trying to remember what had been so all-fired important.

Breathing didn't help. The blood skimming through her veins felt too watery to carry oxygen to her brain. Not that that ever stopped her from arguing before. "Do you have to look at everything in terms of potential disaster?"

"It's safer that way." As if weighing the risks, he studied her face, her eyes, her lips. He reached out. She flinched. He shook his head slightly. To her surprise, she obeyed and held still. He drew a straw out of her hair. "You know, you could poke your eye out with one of these things."

She screamed. "You're impossible!"

"I care about this stuff!"

"And I care about you." She scrambled to her feet.

"Great. I suppose that means you'll come to my room again."

"Not in a million years. I'll drag the bureau over to block the door just in case."

"Fine. You can spend the next three days there enjoying your suspension."

She stormed out of the barn and marched halfway down High Noon Avenue before she realized her blouse was askew, her skirt a mess, and her hair as disheveled as only a hand-clutching, lip-smearing, heart-mangling kiss could make it.

"Who cares!" she hissed, shouldering her way through the swinging doors of the saloon. Her boot heels pounded up the stairs before Bill's and Tony's smirks registered. She swung around. "So I fell off a horse. So I'm filthy, okay?"

They raised their hands in unison, as contrite as if they'd stepped off a stagecoach in the midst of a holdup. "Sorry, Annie."

Her slammed door echoed through the building, trailed by a couple of very male chuckles.

It took Greg half an hour in the shower to wash off the dust, dirt, and dried sweat. He wasted another fifteen minutes in front of the sink reliving the scene in the barn, reproaching the man in the mirror.

"You practically attacked the woman."

Pam would've sent him packing if he'd ever touched her like that. He'd only needed to see fear in her eyes once to keep the rougher aspects of sexuality under rigorous control ever after. Their marriage hadn't lacked passion, but he'd taken it on himself to protect her from the wilder stuff, losing himself in her a thousand nights while never completely losing control. He had never hurt her. He never would. She'd loved him for that reined-in strength, correctly seeing it for what it was, concern and love.

Today had been something else entirely. He'd been

out of hand and out of line. And yet there'd been no fear in Annie at all. He could've sworn she'd been as turned on as he was.

The man in the mirror looked away. "Pretty sorry excuse for mauling a woman."

Greg sank onto the bed, running a hand over the edge of the picture frame. "I thought it was gone," he said aloud. "It all shut down after you—"

He didn't need to complete the sentence. After Pam's death his desire had dried up. He'd expected it to rear its head eventually. But after five years, he'd begun to think he'd never love again, never have to wrestle with such all-consuming desire.

Then Annie Cartwright came along.

He had to get this under control. All of it. His response, his reaction, the physical charge that blind-sided him every time he saw her. She wanted him, that much was clear. She'd stood right there and told him she was the woman for him.

"Well, Pam, this banged-up old cowboy you married ought to be flattered. Maybe some women find faces that look like scarred saddles and wrinkled leather a turn-on.

Pam had.

Annie did.

What was he going to do about it?

"All we've gotta do is set the limits and draw the lines."

Then maybe he could get a decent night's sleep. He left the door open a crack, just in case.

SIX

"All we've gotta do is set the limits and draw the lines."

Annie grinned, her chin resting on her palm as Greg outlined his plan. She half expected him to pull out a pen and diagram it on the paper tablecloth. Then he'd pull out his stopwatch and time it for her.

The cantina rocked with the twang of a country song on the jukebox. The smell of beer and tequila hovered in the cigarette smog.

She stood her spoon in her chili and munched a greasy french fry. Turn the script page and wait for the next cue, she mused. He'd worked everything out except her part. She'd write that.

"What do you think?"

At least he asked. She grinned again. "Sounds as if you've got it all planned. I behave as far as stunts are concerned. You behave as far as sex is concerned." She cleared her throat, then daintily patted her lips with her napkin. "I think we can manage."

He didn't look too comfortable with her dreamy smile and the challenging gaze above it. "By the way, the suspension stands."

She put a fat fry in her mouth, took her time chewing, then licked a salt crystal off her lower lip. She dipped the next fry in a mound of ketchup, twirling it slowly until it was well coated.

He cleared his throat. It sounded like a car in dire need of a tune-up. "You broke a rule of mine. You knew it. You pay the price."

"Okay."

"You aren't going to argue?"

"I'm not even going to throw you across the room. Nope. You're absolutely right. I deserve a twenty-four-hour suspension for shamelessly hotdogging. It's certainly your prerogative as coordinator—"

"Seventy-two hours, Annie."

She never could keep a straight face. "Couldn't slip that one by you, huh?"

"Seventy-two hours. It was blatant."

Blatant covered a lot of things—such as open-mouthed kisses.

Greg's arm shot up. He signaled the waitress for a second beer and another order of fries while Annie polished off hers and brazenly began filching his.

In the charged atmosphere, Annie sipped her ice water. It had certainly gotten hot in there. Almost as bad as the night before.

If one didn't sleep, one didn't sleep*walk*. She'd spent the hours staring at the ceiling, imagining the experience of lying in Greg's bed while he watched her. The fantasy left her body strumming and feverish. The moon impaled the room on its bright shaft, coating her skin like a translucent sheet. She'd idly traced the mole beside her navel, touching where the moon touched and places it hadn't, places Greg might have.

In the cantina, she caught him watching her mouth. Another fry disappeared. "I have a big appetite."

So did he. Thanks to iron self-control, he didn't say it.

Thanks to Annie's imagination, he didn't have to.

They studied their plates.

She was trying to coax him out of his shell, make him live again. But living for Greg Ford involved a strong sexual urge, one that might be too hot for her to handle. Three-alarm chili didn't help. She plucked absently at her blouse. Maybe seventy-two hours apart was a good idea; they could both use a cooling-off period.

"So we draw the line at dinner," she said.

"You have any other ideas?"

A dozen, mostly erotic. "It's safer that way."

"Bingo."

"Tell me about her."

The unexpected question made Greg go still inside. Although Pam was an indelible part of his life, he couldn't remember the last time he'd really talked about her. He mentioned her, of course, a standard version he told new acquaintances. Telling Annie would be different, it might open the wound, or soothe it. He risked it, although he couldn't say why.

"She wasn't anything like you. She was smaller. More delicate."

Annie encouraged him with a self-deprecating smile. "Not a tomboy."

"No. She wore dresses when everyone else wore jeans. She wouldn't leave the house without perfume on. Or a bra."

Annie stopped playing with the third button on her blouse, subtly withdrawing her hand. Greg knew she hadn't meant to be so unconsciously provocative. He felt his body respond all the same.

A sultry wind blew through the desert, trapping the heat. The cantina was close, filled with people. Looking at Annie, the sounds, the smells, the faces faded to a blur. Her hair shimmered in the light of a tin-hatted bulb. His palms itched. He wrapped his hand around a moisture-dotted beer, then wiped the damp across the back of his neck.

It didn't help. He was talking about Pam, not getting worked up over blue eyes and a look that spoke of caring and intense concentration, a look that inadvertently strayed to his mouth, making his heart pound and his lower body tighten and throb.

"What kind of perfume?"

She'd keep him on track. She was that kind of

woman. Pam had been too. "The flowery kind. You don't wear perfume."

"Haven't found any that could compete with the smell of Ben-Gay."

He chuckled with her, recalling the falls he'd seen her take, the bruises on her thigh, the smell of her in his bed. A soft, womanly scent still lingered on his pillow, entwined with the tang of medicinal rub. He pictured smoothing it on for her, smearing it over tanned skin and toned flesh. He'd imagined a lot the last couple of nights, lying awake listening for creaks in the floor.

"Had enough?" He nodded at her empty plate.

All she had to do was nod. He paid the check and they left. On the other side of the swinging doors, he settled his hat on his forehead and tugged it low.

They both needed fresh air. The desert obliged with a surprisingly sultry breeze. It tussled in Annie's hair, sifting ivory strands like beams of moonlight around her face.

Greg looked at the empty heavens. Moonlight and Annie had gotten him in enough hot water. He'd been trying to tell her why he hadn't wanted a woman in the five years since Pam's death. He wasn't supposed to be dreaming up a hundred reasons to change now.

They strolled down the re-created Western street, past a blacksmith's, an apothecary, a dry goods store. Empty storefronts all of them, Hollywood facades.

"I love the way they create a fantasy out of a few boards and paint," she said.

"That and a camera pointed in the right direction."

"Add a few horses, and we're back in the days of cowboys and Indians."

"I used to be a cowboy."

Annie believed him. He had that weather-beaten, wind-scoured look a man got from years living in open spaces. She looked at him and saw prairies, late night rambles under the stars, the most brilliant, bone-thrilling dawns observed through a wary, cautious squint, and she ached for him. No man should be that alone.

"Terrible work," he groused. "Ranches are monasteries with cows. I never stopped smelling like the horse I rode, never got the sand out of my shorts, and lived in a bunkhouse with a bunch of men who smelled as bad as I did."

Annie laughed, the back of her hand brushing against his as they walked. They turned down a street where the facades ended and found themselves on the edge of the desert. The jagged pillars of Monument Valley speared the indigo evening sky. "When did you give it up?"

"When I met Pam," he said.

Annie heard the gentleness in his voice and knew without asking who'd put it there. "She must have been a special woman."

"I suppose any woman you love becomes special."

Annie evaded his look, gazing at the towering stones, lonely and stark. She squeezed his hand and laughed deliberately. "So tell me how she turned a rough and tough cowboy into the paragon of civility I see today."

A curt laugh of his own punctuated the night. "It wasn't what she did, it's what I did because of her. I got a better job on the rodeo circuit, then used the experience to get myself a stunt job. I wanted something steady."

"Seeking out danger isn't exactly a long-term career move."

He shrugged. "Heck, I got off on it as much as anyone does. Showing an angry horse who's boss, wrestling a stock car back onto the track at a hundred miles an hour, crashing on purpose, that was my idea of living. We do crazy things to get that kind of rush. Look at Jackson."

Look at me, Annie thought.

Deep in a memory, Greg broke off a stalk of tumbleweed and crinkled it between his fingers. "For once, I wasn't risking my neck over some dumb bet on the ranch. I had a woman to go home to, a future to plan."

"Then she died."

Over a distant mountain range a star fell, a chalk mark on the sky, quickly erased. Greg winced and turned. They ambled back toward the makeshift town.

"A drunk driver hit her car. She never saw it coming."

"You don't have to go into details if you don't want."

Greg found the details didn't matter. What mattered was that Pam was gone and Annie was there, reaching out.

He took her hand again, his fingers spread so hers could twine with them. Their hands swung between them as they walked. At the end of the street he shook his head. "Anybody watching would think we actually get along."

"We can."

"Is that all you're after?"

"I took one look at you and thought, 'There's a man who needs some excitement in his life.'"

"So you jumped out of a moving car with me."

"I got into one with you." She batted her lashes, earning another laugh.

Greg shook his head. "'Excitement' is as good a word for it as any. About what happened yesterday in the barn, though, I came on way too strong."

"I didn't mind."

"So I noticed."

Barely a breath separated them as they stood, his body close enough to lean into. He kept those scant inches between them. "I wanted to apologize all the same."

"That isn't necessary."

"Then tell me what is."

Her eyes twinkled. "Living. Loving. I know what it is to lose somebody, Greg. It can all be snuffed out so fast. That's why you have to fight back, live as much as you can, don't shut it out."

"Don't shut *you* out?" He touched her cheek with a fingertip, coaxing back a strand of hair.

Everything around them paused, the movement of the air, the rotation of the earth. Small shocks fizzed across her skin.

He closed the gap, his jeans touching hers. The wrinkled cotton of his shirt brushed the silk of hers. The scents of tumbleweed, sage, and sand mixed with the scent of skin, powder on a woman's cheek, a man's shaved chin.

She raised up on her toes and kissed him, showing him the tender, sweet gift love could be. It didn't have to be wild passion. It didn't have to be the end of the world. They could manage to be friends, caring and giving along the way. But how could words alone say all that?

Minutes passed, precious and innocent, her lips lightly teasing his, enticing him out of his shell, out from behind lines and limits that hemmed him in like barbed wire. *Follow me*, she wanted to say.

He barely responded.

Disheartened, she kissed him one last time.

It was one time too many. She should have known she couldn't trust the whisper in her soul urging her to dare more. Her whole life had been stop signs she didn't want to read, yield signs she disobeyed at her own risk.

The pressure of his lips sent a warning; she ignored it. He'd more or less told her he wouldn't be there to catch her if she jumped. Maybe she'd already fallen.

"What do you want from me?" The harshness of his voice echoed his struggle.

"Let this happen," she pleaded.

"I'm not the one stopping." He brushed a kiss across her temple. He nuzzled her neck.

"Give us a chance. If it's meant to be more than friendship—"

"More?" He bit the tender skin below her earlobe.

Her breasts flushed with heat, the sacred place between her legs grew warm and slick with moisture. The area below her navel ached with fullness. She wanted his hand pressed there, his fingers curving downward.

"Risk it," she breathed. "Whatever happens."

He wrapped his arms around her, breathing hard. He said her name, crushed a handful of hair in his fist and rasped the word "Silk." He said the same for her breast when his hand slipped inside her blouse and covered the aching mound.

She arched back, letting it fill his palm. No coyness, no apologies for her lack of frilly lingerie, her modest size. She was willing to risk her body, her spirit, to open completely to a man who'd done nothing more than make some light-headed promise in the heat of passion. Who was taking the real risk here?

Not him, Greg thought.

Crazy ideas rushed into his head, flooding his brain. She was a fine, shining woman, brave and unafraid, a woman who made him want to change his life.

A man would feel a hundred feet tall with someone like Annie beside him.

He wasn't that man. He didn't dance on cliffs anymore. He didn't open his heart to anyone.

He tore away, his muttered curse sounding in the silence that hovered over them.

Annie's gasp died in the air. "What's the matter?"

A string of well-chosen expletives seemed the only appropriate words. Out of the corner of his eye, Greg watched Annie pulling her hair back. Agitated fingers braided it tight.

"Mother used to tell Dad the ranch smelled bad enough without his language stinking up the air too."

His hollow laugh fell flat. She was hurt and he'd done it. Pretending he could love her would be a hundred times worse. "If you want sex, Annie, I'll give it to you, no question. You want more than that."

"More than you're willing to risk, you mean."

He glared at her. She glared right back.

"Okay," he said. "I could lie to you, tell you I'm willing to try anything, when all I really want to do is to make love to you until the sun comes up and the bed caves in. Is that what you want?"

"You know it isn't."

"Which is why you should thank me for stopping now." He marched to the corner of the street. She didn't follow. Twenty abrupt strides brought him back to her. Hell, he couldn't leave a woman standing alone on a deserted street. With a yank he gripped her hand and hauled her toward the hotel.

"We're going to bed. In separate rooms."

Annie collapsed against the inside of her hotel room door, listening as his slammed. She and the striped wallpaper would be cell mates for the next three days while she served her suspension. She sighed and ran a hand over the dented brass bed, the dresser with its basin and jug, a spindleback chair with a cotton T-shirt draped across it. She wadded up the shirt and hurled it into a corner. The sound of falling clothes made for a very unsatisfying tantrum.

She marched into the bathroom and ran the taps full tilt, water thundering in the claw-footed tub. A cup of bubble bath followed. Steam rose. Her muscles craved the relaxing heat, her body the soothing oil, her mind the beautiful view of prisms of color inside mountains of white bubbles. Eventually the bubbles would pop. "All bubbles do," her heart whispered.

Until his few halting words about Pam, Annie hadn't realized how badly Greg's heart had been broken, how rough and ragged the scars still were. "And you stand there and dare him to take a chance."

He wasn't taking it alone. Each time she got close to him, she ended up surrendering in his arms, thrilling to sensations she'd never explored. Unlike Greg, she couldn't pretend they were purely sexual. Falling in love could be the most dangerous fall of all. "No mats, no nets, no cardboard boxes." Just a man's arms to catch her.

She smoothed a handful of foam over her breasts and breathed deep. He'd said he hadn't wanted to make love to a woman since Pam died. "He wants to try. He wants to reach out." *Because he thinks he can keep his emotions out of it.*

Letting her hair slip over the edge of the tub, she sank to her chin, blowing bubbles across the surface of the water. "Let him go back to being lonely," a voice whispered. "Give him his three days." Meanwhile, she had to find a way to ignite his emotions the way she had his libido.

"And if he can't love again?"

She'd pick herself up, dust herself off, and go home. But before that happened, she'd show him risks had payoffs. Harmless flirting could be just that.

"Three days, Mr. Ford. Then I'm making a come-back."

It took two. She ran, she killed time with the crew, she got a hot-oil rinse from the set hairdresser and a facial from the makeup man. In the makeup trailer she chatted with the film's female star, Belinda Saint.

"It makes no sense." The peroxide blonde smacked the script with the backs of her perfectly manicured fingers. "One day I'm a competent career woman, the next a nineteenth-century schoolmarm. How am I supposed to stay in character? No one told me I'd be riding a horse. No one told me I'd have to stand there and let Nicholas Strand hit me!"

The production assistant rapidly explained, the duckbill on his baseball cap bobbing. "It's time travel, see? Career woman inherits ranch, gets thrown by horse, hits head, and goes back in time. People are trying to kill her in both eras."

"I think my agent's trying to kill my career. Mitzi! Mitzi, get Aaron on the phone."

The production assistant rolled his eyes at the name of Belinda's high-powered agent.

"Have you read this?" Belinda asked Annie.

Annie shrugged. "They throw me out of cars and off tall buildings. I never read the script."

Belinda smirked, careful not to crease her makeup with an actual smile. "Neither do I, that's what agents are for."

"You don't have to get slapped for real, you know."

"Nicholas has this wonderful way of slipping up and actually landing one. He's very apologetic afterward. Says it has nothing to do with our affair on the last movie we made."

Annie recalled her conversation with Greg regarding movie-set romances. She'd promised herself seventy-two hours to cool off. On the other hand, she had a skill that was called for. "I can do it."

"Do what?" Belinda asked.

"Take a slap. Not a real one, but my timing is great. I can duck anything he dishes out."

"That would drive Nicholas wild. You're coming

with me. Mitzi! Call Costuming, get her an outfit like mine. Annie, right? What century are we in in this next scene?"

They walked into a nineteenth-century saloon. Cowboys lined the bar. A piano sat silent but well lit in a corner. Whiskey glasses and spittoons littered a sawdust-covered floor. Ten feet away camera cables tangled on the planking while reflectors and booms clustered overhead.

Greg knew the minute she came on the set. All heads turned toward Belinda, America's latest platinum sweetheart. He wouldn't be a man if he hadn't been aware of the famous cleavage a nasty tabloid had dubbed Silicon Valley. Let everyone else stare. The woman beside the star stole his breath away.

Annie wore the same dancehall dress. Her hair was naturally white-blond, her face oval, her eyes softer blue. Vibrant, not blasé, she radiated an aura of energy. She loved her work; it showed. What else did she love?

Annie gave him a shrug before venturing over. "You said I couldn't work. You didn't say I couldn't watch."

Greg glowered at his stopwatch. "You aren't in this stunt."

"The action starts when Belinda gets slapped. She wanted me to take it for her."

Belinda flashed him a smile. "Any problems here?"

He couldn't very well argue with the director's latest flame. "Take it," he said to Annie. "You can serve out the third day later."

"Anything you say, boss. And boss?" She got up on her tiptoes.

He jumped back as if she'd tried handing him a scorpion. "No hugs, no kisses, no thank-you's."

Thoroughly contrite, she compressed her lips and clasped her hands behind her back. Unfortunately, that forced her breasts against the lace edging of her low-cut dress. "I'll be quiet as a mouse."

He muttered something as he walked away. It sounded suspiciously like, "I'll believe it when I see it."

"Howdy."

Annie whirled, grinning at the first person she saw—Jackson, the hotheaded young stuntman.

"Heard you got suspended too," he said. "He's a real tightass about rules."

"I think he's got your best interests at heart."

"Has he got yours yet?" The young man rubbed the lace outlining her bodice between his fingers.

Annie would have been insulted if he hadn't been so young. He reminded her of Cody, all hormones and Harleys. She lifted his hand away. Glancing up, she caught Greg deep in conversation with the second-unit director. She could have sworn he'd been watching. Something about the way the tension in his shoulders climbed halfway up his neck.

She chuckled. "Sorry, Jackson. I'm waiting for the

star." She nodded at Nicholas Strand as he made his entrance.

"What do women see in him?"

"I honestly don't know."

The man was as cosmetically perfect as Belinda Saint. He played his suave image twenty-four hours a day. When Belinda introduced them, he bowed at the waist, kissing Annie's hand. "Charmed."

Once more Annie thought she caught a movement out of the corner of her eye. It was only Greg crashing a breakaway chair over a stuntman's back as he walked the crew through the coming scene.

Nicholas jumped at the racket.

Annie grinned tightly. "Don't mind him. They'll do this a million times to get it right."

"Mm. Love scenes are the same way. Over and over."

Annie waited for a blush, a flush, any kind of response at all. After all, Strand had been officially named one of the sexiest men alive not two years earlier. She'd heartily agreed at the time. She hadn't known Greg Ford then. "Shall we work on our scene?"

Flustered by her lack of interest, Strand nodded. "By all means."

Greg spent hours rehearsing a scene that took place in every Western ever made. Nevertheless, he remained impervious to the production assistant's pleas for haste. Crew members squared off, raising bottles they'd smash over each other's heads, hefting break-away chairs, swinging rights and lefts and uppercuts that never landed but always snapped heads back and doubled large men over. They would run through the entire fight in one master shot, then restage pieces of it for closeups. Greg had everything under control and ready to roll. The slap resounded across the set.

Annie clutched the bar rail with one hand. The other trembled as she covered her cheek with it. Strand stood there, upright, indifferent, smug. "That didn't hurt, did it?"

Greg's gut clenched. He strode onto the set, the stopwatch practically crushed in his grip. He stopped a foot from Strand. He scanned Annie's cheek. No hand mark, no redness. "What happened?"

Annie blanched at his brusque tone. "Making it look real."

"Wait over there. I'll call you when we need you." She marched off.

Strand tried to be helpful. "I can do it better. When she isn't expecting it, you know?"

Greg looked him up and down, his voice low. "You hit her for real, and I'll kill you. Got that?"

He didn't wait for an answer.

Greg sank into his seat in the makeshift viewing room. The rushes captured a flawless melee. The only fault anyone found with the uncut film was the morti-fied look on Nicholas Strand's face.

"Was he constipated or what?" The production assistant made a note. Tomorrow's closeups would remedy the problem.

Greg wasn't sure anything could cure *his* problem. He cared about Annie, deep down in his gut, in places he'd walled off a long time ago. Getting her off the set only taught him how capable he was of missing her.

He asked to see the film again and again, keeping his eye on the blonde at the bar. Strand slapped her. She flinched at exactly the right moment. Playacting, fantasy, Greg should have known. Dammit if he didn't care.

SEVEN

He was grumpy as a bear all week. Keeping as far from Annie as humanly possible had been a fine strategy. Suspending her even better. Now if someone would clue her in on it.

She teased him mercilessly, pestering him with awful jokes, giving him sidewinder hugs, brushing flirtatiously past him, always when he most needed it and least expected it. Every time he happened to think of her and looked up, she caught him, a Mona Lisa smile flitting across her face.

"Women." Growling did no good.

A week of her attention and he'd grown to expect it, anticipating her arrival, flipping through the script to her next stunt, listening for the sound of a bath running across the hall from his room, picturing her lowering herself into it, then into his bed. Why not? Fantasies were free.

And time was money. She'd totally disrupted his work, his life, and his crew. Her sense of fun infected every one of them. Bill saw to it she never missed a briefing. Chris and Antony came up with suggestions for new stunts she could do. They got a kick out of seeing their boss squirm.

He wasn't beat yet. Poked, prodded, and bullied into living again, he'd dig his heels in and fight every last one of them, starting with Annie. Two could play this game.

He spread the diagram for the explosion scene on the folding table set up outside the trailer. Like a genie, Annie materialized. Two minutes more and he could have suspended her for tardiness. No such luck.

"Hi, guys."

"Hi, Annie."

The men squeezed shoulder to shoulder to give her room—right beside Greg.

His expression grim, he drew their attention to the area they'd have to secure before setting the explosives. "The scene involves a Corvette, a load of plastic explosives, blasting caps, gasoline, and a few sticks of good old TNT. We don't want so much sand flying, you can't see the flames. On the other hand, we don't want to turn this into a ton of shrapnel and melted fiberglass. Jack, you want to go over it?"

While the demolitions expert stepped in to explain the volatile mix, Greg inhaled the sharp morning air. He casually reached toward his back pocket.

"Ouch!" Annie let out a yip. Freezing on tiptoe, she clamped a hand to her backside.

Greg calmly retrieved a pencil, making a notation on the shooting script. "Any questions?"

The men pursed their lips and shook their heads, peering at the map, peeking at Annie's burning cheeks.

That left two cheeks unaccounted for, Annie thought. One of them still twinged from the expert pinch he'd delivered. When the crew received their final instructions and dispersed, she sidled up to Greg. "Some people would call that sexual harassment, *boss*."

He chuckled to himself, flipping the pages of the script.

"Add insensitivity to the charge."

"Your behind is very sensitive. I'll keep that in mind. You don't really object, do you?"

This playful side of him was new. She deeply distrusted it. "And if I did object?"

"You'd have tossed me across that table, and we both know it."

He had her there. Annie muttered something about violence not being the answer for everything. She stuck her hand in her back pocket, rubbing vigorously. "It's probably a bruise."

"Want me to kiss it and make it better?"

"No!"

The tiger she'd teased had escaped his cage, and she didn't like the way he was grinning at her. She whirled on her heel, giving him a good long look at her derriere as she flounced down the street. At least she'd have the final word. "As a matter of fact, kissing it is *exactly* what you can do."

Greg's rumbling laugh declared the encounter a tie.

He pondered his next move while waiting behind the grocer's facade. Annie had been running and riding him for a week. For the last two days she'd run and ridden *away* from *him*. He must be doing something right. Besides, seeing her off balance for a change was fun. Scheming to keep her that way gave him a reason to bound out of bed every morning.

It took two to argue, two to tango. From Eden to the ark, the world was made for twos. Except in stunt work. You could never pull the same gag twice. What could he do next?

His pulse sped up at the sound of her striding down the sidewalk. Heels snapping, she walked her straight-ahead tomboy walk. He waited until she reached the edge of the alley, then, with split-second timing, yanked her around the corner and into his arms.

Emotions raced across her face faster than a summer storm—shock, anger, readiness to fight. Her whole body tensed. Then she recognized him. A touch of alarm widened her eyes, a hint of happy surprise colored her cheeks. Beneath it all, undeniable currents of sexual excitement simmered.

He lost it. Whatever momentum he'd had evaporated. It wasn't a joke. It wasn't a game. In the striped shadows cast by struts and plywood, he knew what he'd been waiting for. He kissed her. Hard.

Annie closed her eyes. She didn't need them. Her nose recognized the spicy scent of his cologne, her mouth the peppermint of his toothpaste, her body the breadth of his shoulders, the heat of him pressed to her.

This kiss was no tease. It wasn't angry, unless a badger teased out of its hole was angry. It wasn't demanding, unless the absolute need of a man for a woman was demanding. It wasn't dangerous, unless falling in love was dangerous.

She desperately reminded herself he'd kissed her before, frankly passionate, brutally indiscreet. The erotic honesty thrilled and frightened her, sending warnings to every corner of her surrendering body. He wanted sex; she wanted love. If she wanted to protect some small corner of her soul, she had to remember that.

They broke apart at the sound of laughter on the other side of the facade. Breathing hard, they stared at each other.

"Good thing I have split-second reflexes, or you'd be flat on your back, Ford."

"After the way you've teased me all week, the only surprise is I didn't do it sooner." He lifted a lock of her hair, nuzzling her neck. "Recognized me, huh?"

"That has more to do with a woman's instincts than a stuntwoman's."

"Always obey your instincts." He skimmed her neck again.

The breath left her body. Her bones turned to rubber.

"You don't have to think to feel this," he said. "This is what it would be like, me inside you. Like silk."

Annie didn't know how to take his unexpected gentleness. She only knew she couldn't resist it. Her willpower dissolved. Her body blossomed when he touched her.

His husky voice rasped across the silence. "Come to my room later."

She almost said yes.

A horn honked. Bill and Amos sat in a Jeep at the end of the alley, staring straight ahead, their cowboy hats pulled low.

Playing with her blouse, her hair, she finally shoved her hands in the front pockets of her jeans and struck a casual pose. She hadn't meant any of that—not the way she'd wrapped her arms around his neck, nor opened her mouth, not let her tongue undulate with his.

Or so she wanted him to think.

"Coming, boss?" Amos called.

"If he only knew," Greg murmured.

Her eyes widened by a fraction. Her crooked smile felt as forced as his looked. He reached out a finger to touch her cheek. It took every ounce of courage she had not to run. She sensed he knew that, and saw that he admired it. "Greg—"

"I'll make it easy on both of us." He walked away.

"This is another fine mess you've gotten us into." Frowning, Annie lowered herself into a bubble bath hot enough to poach eggs. She'd be as wrinkled as a white prune when she got out.

She'd be ninety before she figured out Greg Ford. Just when she'd thought him safely gone, he'd spoken a few terse words to Bill and Amos, waved the Jeep away, and returned. She'd been riveted to the spot. Her mind yelled, "Run." Her arms rose of their own volition.

He'd whipped off his hat and swept an arm around her waist, bending her back. His good-bye kiss had sizzled like a snake on a hot rock. Behind her closed eyes, she remembered heat and glaring sun, an inferno trapped within. She'd emerged breathless and mussed into the bright light of day. Around a corner the Jeep backfired. Greg put on his hat and left without a word.

"Oh, Annie." Why did she have to leap into life with both feet? She squelched a pile of bubbles with her toes. "Stop and think next time."

Think what? He made her feel, up and down her spine, inside and out, feelings that whispered through her at night. Her dreams, waking and sleeping, were filled with images of one man, unexplored yearnings. It sounded an awful lot like love—as corny as a golden oldie and as real as the ground beneath her.

Her backside squeaked against the porcelain tub. She felt the faint bruise left by his pinch. She laughed.

She wanted to cry. Nothing made sense. He ran, she wanted to run after him. He came after her, she turned and ran. Or stayed and held on for dear life.

She was falling, all right. "Just remember to land on your feet."

Greg grumbled hello to the two stray crew members lounging in the location trailer and helped himself to a cold one from the fridge. For the hundredth time that week he found himself worrying, obsessing, and fantasizing about a woman.

"Where's Annie?" Jackson leaned in the doorway, cocky and lazy all at once.

"She's on the main set shooting close-ups."

The young stuntman let the screen slam shut.

Greg glanced at his watch. They'd be shooting over-the-shoulder angles of Nicholas Strand slapping Annie. The idea set Greg's teeth on edge. So did the ice-cold beer. He gulped half the can. What was the worst that could happen? If Strand didn't give her time to flinch, if his palm connected—

"Boss, you're supposed to crush the cans *after* you drink the beer."

He glared at Chris and Tony and poured the rest down the sink. "You slugs got anything better to do besides waste your break on my couch?"

"Just waitin' for Annie."

He banked the mangled can into the wastebasket. "Why?"

"She said she'd buy us lunch after we blow up the car."

" 'Those of us still in one piece,' she said."

Greg recognized Annie's gallows humor. She fit in perfectly. She'd been all but born to it.

So why couldn't he stop worrying about her? He stared out the window, checking on Jack setting the explosives under a shiny new Corvette. He remembered the paint job they'd put on the car they'd driven over the cliff to make it look newer. He'd held Annie in his arms in that lumpy backseat. Shocks had trembled through him as he held a woman again, sensations he hadn't felt in years. All because of her.

"Chris. Go see how long Jack's going to take with that plastic. And if the ProdAss catches you, tell him I'm out to lunch."

"He'll believe that." Chris meandered out the door toward the demolitions expert.

Greg mentally reviewed the stunt. When the car blew, Jackson would leap toward the camera as if thrown by the force of the blast. He'd have to wear a flak vest in case of flying debris.

Details. How many times had he used them to avoid thinking about the past, feeling it? Details had gotten him through the worst of his grief. The grief faded. Now what?

Try again. The words whispered near his heart. But was the woman's voice Pam's or Annie's?

He strode into the suffocating noon heat. Scowling, he pulled his hat low on his forehead. He could maybe take her out on a date. Kiss her some. More than that. Maybe he could give living another try.

Hell, if she had any idea he even entertained the thought, she'd probably flap her arms and crow. On the other hand, what did he have to lose?

The production assistant waved his cellular phone in one hand, the script in the other, his shrill voice echoing across the location. "You mean to tell me we lost a silver 1993 Corvette convertible with dual cams, super-reinforced suspension, and a CD player that cost more than my first house? Is that what you're telling me? Is it?"

Impassive as stone, Greg nodded. "Look for yourself."

The production assistant didn't bother with the twisted wreckage behind him, squeezing the life out of the phone in his hand. "How are we going to explain to the studio exec who *loaned* us this car, that you blew up his brand new Corvette? Huh? Huh?"

Annie gulped. The crew inched their way backward. Like a man standing court-martial, waiting to have his stripes ripped from his shoulders, Greg stared straight ahead. The director himself had helicoptered in to view the wreckage. Standing behind reflecting sunglasses, in the shade cast by the bill of his baseball cap, Lucas Stone left the screaming to his production assistant.

"Do you have any idea," the little man screeched,

"how much that car cost? Do you have any idea who *owned* it?"

Greg clenched his jaw and shook his head.

"The controller! The man who pays the bills. The man who pays *your* check!"

Annie winced sympathetically, silently sending Greg what support she could. Somehow this was all her fault. Somehow they'd let the shiny new automobile sit there atop a platform loaded with explosives and no one had thought to bring on the replacement before pushing the button.

She'd gotten back just before they'd shot the scene. Greg was busy seeing to details, checking his watch, worrying about Jackson hotdogging on this one. The young man had some kind of crush on her and seemed to think he'd prove his stuff by wearing as little protection as possible. Seeing Greg about to blow his stack, Annie moseyed up to the young man and slid her arm through his.

"You know," she'd said, her voice as throaty as she could make it without coughing or busting out laughing, "in this day and age, a man should *always* use protection. Believe me, a lady appreciates it."

The rest of the crew choked back their laughter as Annie sidled over to Greg. "He'll wear it," she murmured under her breath.

Focusing on the diagram spread before him, Greg replied without raising his voice. "I don't think he'll know how neatly you cut him off at the knees until he tries to take his boots off tonight and his legs come off with 'em."

"Just trying to be helpful."

"Thanks."

She'd soared on that one word for the next fifteen minutes. The cameras were in place. Jackson took his mark. The car blew up precisely and impeccably. Flames shot thirty feet in the air. A patter of dirt and dust rained down in a neatly proscribed arc. The explosion reduced the chassis to twisted metal vines twining around bucket seats. Perfect, really, if only it hadn't been—

"—the wrong car!"

Greg broke his thousand-mile stare and looked the production assistant in the eye. "What do you want me to do about it?"

The vein on the little man's pink scalp nearly popped. "Get another one! We have scenes to shoot. Scenes that require a drivable, recognizable automobile!"

"Okay. We'll get another."

"It isn't that simple!"

Wasn't it? No one had said the words "You're fired" or "You'll never work in this town again"; that meant they could work this out. "I'll take one of the crew, we'll drive over to L.A. and pick up a new car."

"From who? Who on the studio lot is going to be stupid enough to loan you a vehicle when you blew up the controller's car?"

"I could always borrow yours."

From the way his mouth clamped shut, Annie thought the assistant would blow up more spectacularly than the car had.

Greg scanned the crowd. His eyes lit on Annie. "We'll be back by Thursday. If I don't have another car, I don't have a job. Deal?"

"You don't have a car, you don't have a *career*."

"Excuse the mess. Don't carry too many passengers in this thing." Greg threw a notepad, maps, sunglasses, and a fistful of old speeding tickets behind the bench seat of the pickup truck. After Annie climbed in, got settled, and smiled his way, he retrieved the sunglasses. "It's gonna be a long drive."

He was usually so organized, Annie expected a checklist of things to take on a trip. Instead, he'd thrown a few clothes in a sports bag and knocked on her hotel room door. "We've got a fourteen-hour drive. We can go all night, or we can find a motel around the California border and get to L.A. in the morning."

Stay in a motel with Greg Ford? Annie threw up her hands, realizing too late that the shaking showed. "You're the boss."

"We'll stop at Needles."

They drove south to Flagstaff and across Arizona. Tex Mex music twanged from the radio. Greg squinted at the unchanging horizon, the flat stretch of road, and drove.

Annie studied the dusty dashboard. His pickup

truck was as battered as his heart. Numerous dents gave the body texture, hinting at the rough paths it had crossed. A sinuous crack, flat and white, ribboned across the windshield from right to left. Annie loved the smell of split vinyl and musty carpeting, the mannish scent of an old leather jacket slung over the seat between them.

"That was some explosion," she said after one hundred miles of silence.

"Yep."

"Kind of exciting."

"Right."

"Kind of embarrassing."

"Very."

Kind of like love, she thought morosely. "Mistakes happen."

"Not when I'm around."

"And they do when I am?"

"So far that seems to be the pattern. A stuck door on a car flying off a mountain, an unrehearsed fall from a horse, a car I forgot to substitute—"

"What makes that *my* fault?"

"The fact I couldn't get you out of my mind, that's what."

It was the closest he'd come to admitting any feelings beyond physical ones. Annie was too steamed to care. "Is that why you brought me along, to yell at me?"

"Nope."

"Then why?"

"I need someone to sweet-talk an executive into giving us a car. I can't swish my hair the way you can."

So much for feelings! A strangled scream escaped her. Seat-belted in, she twisted tightly around, grabbing his empty jacket. Hissing a well-earned expletive, she crumpled it behind her head for a pillow. "Mind if I take a nap?"

"Nope."

If eyelids could snap closed, hers had.

For the next hundred miles Greg gripped the leather wheel cover and stared straight ahead, probing his feelings as if they were a sore tooth. He'd managed to put her out of his mind for a full five minutes while working on that stunt. Then he'd given the signal to roll cameras. Tony had run around the corner of the stable, waving his arms and shouting. Too late. The car blew, the explosion rocking the earth beneath Greg's feet.

His mind raced. Before the patter of jagged metal and sand finished raining down on the parched ground, a dozen possibilities marauded through his mind. Jackson seemed fine. Everyone else stayed well back. *Where was Annie?*

Greg's head had pivoted sharply, his heart a jackhammer in his chest. She'd been there a minute ago, wearing a brassy little shorts outfit. It had been all he could do to keep his mind on business. *Where was she?*

He spotted her taking cover beside the trailer. Their eyes met, giving away more emotion than they'd been able to speak. Only then did his heart resume beating, only when he knew she was safe.

Tony's words finally penetrated. They'd blown up the wrong car.

Despite the mix-up and the public dressing-down, his adrenaline had yet to level off. He'd chosen Annie to come with him because he cared about her more than he cared to admit. The fact that he didn't have the guts to do anything about it, ate at him.

He wanted a woman in his life, this woman. He wanted to make love to her, but he couldn't promise to love her. He honestly didn't know if he was capable of loving anymore.

Later when they reached the motel, he'd ask her to meet him more than halfway. Something had burned between them since the day they'd met. It was time to test the fire.

It wasn't much to offer. He knew she wanted more. The voice in his heart said, "*Try*." This time he listened.

EIGHT

"What is this, a cactus convention? There's gotta be a vacancy in Needles." They cruised past another parking lot lined with palm trees and campers while Greg muttered to himself.

Annie slurped the last of her vanilla shake and folded the map. "Twelve miles and turn right."

"You know a place?"

"My daddy's ranch." She'd plotted for two hundred miles how to avoid staying in a motel with Greg Ford. Separate rooms were the obvious answer. The obvious reply; no way. All he had to do was ask and she'd be in his arms, and they both knew it.

So why was she avoiding it?

He'd been very honest about wanting her, all the while claiming he couldn't give her any more than a physical relationship. Horsefeathers. She'd seen the way he'd searched for her in the seconds following the explosion, the look in his eyes when he'd found her.

"I love you too," she thought silently.

But what if he never said it? What if he stubbornly clung to what was right there in his arms and never dared go further, to open his emotions to her? Staying at the Cartwright ranch offered them one more night to talk, one last chance to discover if he could ever return her feelings, if he'd ever risk it.

Studying the stubborn set of his shoulders, she thought the words she couldn't say. "You've been thrown, stomped on, and darn near had the stuffing kicked out of you. Get back on that horse and ride it, Ford. For me. For her, if you have to. Just don't give up."

His heart had been badly damaged. That didn't mean it had stopped beating. Even this battered old truck runs, she thought. Stuffing the map in the glove compartment, she let the rickety old pickup take them home.

Dust off the drive settled around them as they pulled to a stop in front of the weathered ranch house. The sound of the truck engine drifted to earth with the dust. A living room lamp cast a beam of yellow light onto the porch. A yard light out back shone on a half dozen outbuildings. A skeletal windmill sawed and creaked in a halfhearted breeze. No dogs barked. No crickets chirped.

"No one home," Annie said. Her heart sank. She stepped down from the truck. A breath of heat swirled across her ankles, working its way up her skin.

Greg hung back, his fingers dawdling on the door handle. "Maybe we should have called."

Annie forced a smile, teasing him out of his discomfort and hers. "Worried about meeting my father?"

"Looks as if your chaperon isn't around," he murmured.

He'd seen through her plan. The minute he shut the door with a clang and ambled around the front of the truck, she knew she was in trouble.

"He won't be long; he wouldn't have left the light on." She danced up onto the porch, vainly rattling the doorknob.

"Want me to kick it in?"

"No!" No doubt he knew how. He was also expert at making her pulse race and her good sense crumble.

Crowding her on the porch, he tilted his head toward the swing. "I suggest we sit down."

"Why?" Her voice was all breath, catching like cloth on barbed wire.

"We've got to talk. You and me—" He let his hand complete the sentence, tracing her face in the shadowy light. "We've been moving kind of fast."

"Like a freight train."

"If I'm scaring you off—"

"I don't scare easy."

"So I noticed. Every time I think you're gone for good, you come back stronger."

Fortunately, he couldn't hear the slamming of her heart or detect the faint quaver in her words. "Sheer cussedness, I guess."

"Or maybe you like me?"

"No maybe about it."

"Want to do something about it?"

"We can talk."

"I had something else in mind."

"Don't I know it!" Yanking his wrist, she sat him beside her on the swing.

Greg planted his boot heel, rocking them back and forth. He stretched an arm around her, his fingers squeezing in rhythm with their sway. He felt so warm, so solid. His body smelled like sage and leather, familiar scents with a hint of spice. Inch by inch, Annie relaxed into him. Her hand strayed onto his chest, revealing the wild card of his heartbeat, so erratic compared to his steady, soothing presence. She sat up straight and notched her fingers together in her lap.

He urged her into the crook of his arm, his chin caressing the crown of her head. His chest expanded as he inhaled her potpourri of fragrances, shampoo, scented soap. His breath, sweet and warm, tantalized her ear. She nearly purred. A tiny flicker deep inside lit her from within. The reassuring scent of his cheek, a soft kiss, these she could handle. These she loved. Any more and she'd be lost.

She fidgeted, discouraging his fingers as they strummed the side of her neck. "We'll wait an hour."

"And if he isn't back by then?"

"We can talk." Get her started and Annie could talk till the moon turned blue. "You can time it with your stopwatch."

"Left it on location."

With the picture of Pam? The question pierced her like the keen point of a dart. Was that what bothered her, what suddenly held her back? She loved living, taking everything to the max. She didn't know how to compete with a ghost. She couldn't give him what Pam had.

She reluctantly withdrew. But the play of light and dark across his face drew her. She touched the etchings of time and pain. "You've had as many sleepless nights over this as I have."

"One more. You slept through that night in my bed."

She laughed softly. "Doesn't sound too complimentary, does it? It wasn't on purpose, Greg."

"Another blow to my ego. I'd like to think some part of you knew what you were doing. They say dreams are wish fulfillment. Maybe you wanted me so bad—" His hand flitted past the mound of her breast and came to rest on her waist.

Only then did she exhale. She was growing light-headed waiting for him to make a move. And loving every crazy minute.

She crossed her legs, her ankle inadvertently brushing his shin. "Unfortunately, this personality has scared away more men that you'd ever guess."

"I'll bet."

"That was supposed to elicit sympathy."

"Poor tomboy longs to wear frilly dresses and be treated like a princess. Was that the song you were playing?"

"Maybe."

"Hey, I've seen you rolling in the dirt. Heck, I tossed you in some hay myself."

"More floor than hay."

"I told you I'd kiss the bruises and make them better."

Her breath caught again. "That'd only make it worse."

"Worth a try."

He snuck a kiss, a quick reminder they were alone. Then a longer, deeper reminder of how much night stretched before them. Coyotes silently watched from the hills. The moon wore a cloud as if it were an eyepatch. The windmill creaked in time to the swing.

Annie's mouth opened under his fervent pressure. Her fingers raced up his thigh, splaying across his abdomen. She pulled back, breathless. "Are we making bruises or healing them?"

"That's up to you. You said you like it rough."

"I like passion. To hold back is—to hold back. Emotionally, I mean." The words rushed out. She hadn't meant to say it so baldly. "It's the same with work, Greg. Once you're committed, you can't second-guess; you have to go for it, absolutely convinced you can't fail."

"This isn't a stunt."

"It's a risk."

He recognized her dauntlessness. She wanted emotions from him he wasn't sure existed anymore. For years he hadn't even wanted to love again. What if he tried and couldn't? What if his ability to love had died with Pam?

The moon emerged stealthy and white from behind its cloud.

"I don't want to promise you anything I can't deliver."

"I'm not asking for promises. Give us a chance. That's all. Try."

"Try again, you mean."

She didn't flinch, his brave, dare-anything Annie. "Do you still love her?"

Why couldn't he answer that? He leaned forward, elbows balanced on his knees, and worked a fist against the palm of his hand. A knuckle broken long ago ached reassuringly, a manageable pain. "For a long time I thought Pam was all the love I'd ever have. If I stopped loving her, there'd be nothing left."

He looked out over the yard. The silvery light on a sagebrush could have been a woman's scarf or a siren's silvery hair.

"I've lost people too." Her fingertips stroked the back of his neck.

"I'm sorry about Cody, but it isn't the same. Don't get me wrong, but we don't have much choice in family. When you find someone out of the whole world, someone to spend your life with, it's different."

He cursed and sat back. Annie gave him the space he needed.

"I was so damned cocky. I came up with one crazy stunt after another, proving I could be more than a hired hand on some ranch. I took risks for a living, made myself a reputation. I wanted to make her proud of me."

"I'm sure she was."

"But it was all about me. Me getting hurt. Me taking the chances. I never thought for a moment she'd be the one." He squinted at the square of light, then the darkness.

"She probably hurt every time you came home with a scratch," Annie said.

He slouched again, running a hand over his face. "Women."

She prodded him in the ribs. "Get used to it."

"I've tried."

Some things were harder to get over than others. Annie left the thought unsaid. She ran a hand up his spine where he'd hunched his shoulders, kneading the knotted muscle at the base of his neck. He tiredly ran a hand over the same spot, rubbing his neck hard, tangling his fingers with hers. She thought he'd stop her. Instead he brought her palm to his lips and kissed it. Something sweet uncurled inside her. The lump in her throat tightened.

"I don't want you falling in love with me," he said hoarsely.

"That's a risk I have to take."

He shook his head. "It's my responsibility too. You've been chasing me all over creation, and believe me, I've noticed."

"Good. I considered swinging a two-by-four at the back of your head if you didn't sit up and pay attention soon."

"You think I need you."

"You need a woman."

"Isn't that rather old-fashioned?"

"Old-fashioned because it's been true for a few thousand years."

"A man needs a mate, huh?"

"A man needs someone to make him laugh, maybe make him hurt, definitely pull him up short when he gets full of himself."

"Crack the whip."

She gave him a cocky smile. "Well, if you want to get kinky—"

"And you're that woman."

"There won't be another Pam," she replied, a whisper of reality intruding.

He could take it. He turned it around, looking at the practical side. "There are five guys on the set right now with the hots for you. You could have any one of them."

"And I'm stuck with you. Perverse, isn't it?"

"I don't want you falling in love—"

Annie jumped up. "Too late. Daddy's home."

A van turned in at the end of the drive. She waved gaily as it swung to a halt at the dark end of the porch.

Greg took his place beside her, eager to get this said before her old man got out of the van. "I can't promise you anything."

"I never asked."

The darn woman had more pride than sense. "I could lie," he added, "promise it'll work out."

"Could."

"Has any man ever lied to get you in bed, Annie?"

Her waving hand stuttered in the air. Even in this light her cheeks colored. "One."

Greg considered that for a beat. "Bet he didn't walk straight for a month."

It would have been funny if it hadn't been so right on. Did he know her *that* well?

She riveted her attention on the van. She knew better than to wait for the driver's door to open. The side swung wide and a whirring sound filled the interior. A metal grate lowered and a wheelchair rolled onto it. The lift descended, bringing Rusty Cartwright's wheelchair even with the ground.

Greg gripped Annie's arm as she led him down the ramp, his voice tense and accusatory. "You never told me he'd been paralyzed in a stunt."

"Arthritis got him," she replied. "Years of breaks and sprains add up. Hi, Dad."

The old man propelled himself forward. "See you brought another cowboy home."

Annie gave her father a peck on the cheek and straightened, not so accidentally bumping Greg with a sassy sway of her hips. "How'd you guess?"

"You can take 'em out of the bunkhouse but you can't take the bunkhouse out of them." The old man jabbed a finger at his other cheek.

Annie stepped smartly to the other side and kissed him there. Then she took her place at the handles and pushed. She huffed and puffed up the ramp, all of it for show. "Put on a few pounds, Dad?"

"Eating my own cooking? Hardly." He shoved a key in the front door, then pointed the way to the kitchen like the redoubtable prow of an ancient schooner. "Refrigerator. Dead ahead."

Under the gleaming fluorescent of the overhead light, her father swung around, examining Greg minutely.

Standing, the old man would have been over six feet. His hair was iron gray, bristly and close cropped, his skin creased and crinkled. His eyes twinkled blue and sharp, just like Annie's but not as friendly. "Now that I can see him, does your cowboy have a name?"

Annie blew a loose strand of hair off her forehead and set her hands on her hips. "Greg, I'd like you to meet my father, Rusty Cartwright. Dad, I'd like you to meet Greg Ford."

"Name sounds familiar."

"Don't go giving him that evil eye. He's a stuntman too."

"Is he now?" The old man brightened considerably. His crushing handshake engulfed Greg's.

Greg knew a test when he felt one. Released, he

resisted the urge to wave the cramp out of his hand. "Stunt coordinator now, sir."

Annie winked at Greg. "He's in charge of the picture I'm working on, Dad."

"Smart girl," Rusty retorted. "Knows how to keep a job."

"Very funny. I'm earning every last penny and I've got the bruises to prove it. What've you got in the fridge?" She sniffed a package of steak cubes with a disdainful wrinkle of her nose and commenced tossing a variety of vegetables onto the counter. "Since we arrived starving and uninvited, how about me making us some stew?"

Rusty grumbled about life on location and the box lunches the studio provided. "This young man probably doesn't know what a good cook my girl is. Do you, sonny?"

"Sonny?" Annie mouthed the word in mock horror. "If you're going to play the old coot, I'll mix Geritol in your milk."

Rusty shrugged. "You want a feisty widower, a crusty old rancher, or a broken-down rodeo rider, I'm your man."

Annie kissed him again. "Try the lovable old cuss with the heart of gold."

"Character acting for when I couldn't do stunts anymore," he explained to Greg. "Clichés, all of 'em. Nothing but typecasting. Guess they know an old coot when they see one."

This last sentence was spoken in stereo with Annie.

Greg leaned back and watched. Father and daughter set the table with the choreographed efficiency and practiced banter of an old vaudeville team.

"Acting's too easy," Rusty said, a pile of plates clinking on his lap as he glided by Greg into the dining room. "I was always proudest of my stunt work."

"I'd bet Annie made you prouder."

Annie whooped from the kitchen. "He's all flattery, Dad."

"You got that right." Rusty gave Greg a sidelong look his daughter couldn't see, pride puffing out his chest. The thin smile beneath his crusty expression said it all.

Annie chopped green peppers at the sink. "Is that male bonding I hear?"

Rusty chuckled. "You haven't heard the sound of beer tops popping, have you?"

"You haven't shown him the pictures of Cody yet, either."

"There's an idea. Get the beer, son."

Annie shooed Greg away as he fished two out of the refrigerator. "You and Rollalong Cassidy git. I'll finish the stew."

He reached around her, circling a surprisingly delicate wrist with his hand, stilling the flashing knife. "I like him," he murmured.

She turned, her face so close, their lips almost met. "I think he likes you."

It mattered. Greg heard it in her voice. It didn't surprise him that he recognized her unspoken emotions. He'd been watching her too long not to know her expressions intimately.

But something else bothered her; she didn't want him to see. It surprised him to his soul and back how much he wanted her to share those doubts with him, whatever they might be.

Under the circumstances, he could only promise her one thing. "I'll be back." In the living room, he paused before a photograph of Rusty and Cody at a rodeo.

"So you're a stuntman, eh?"

Greg gave the older man a frank look. "The only stunts I do nowadays are ones I wouldn't ask my crew to do."

"Like riding down mountains in out-of-control cars? They've got phones in those location towns."

"I didn't know she'd been reporting in. Guess she's mentioned me."

The old man gave him a "wouldn't you like to know" grin.

Greg stepped along to the next case of trophies and ribbons. Rusty continued the tour.

"That's Cody at sixteen. Then me the same age. If you're looking for a family resemblance, you'd have to see a picture of Annie's Ma." He directed Greg to a silver frame on a dusted piano.

"She was very pretty." The truer resemblance was in the spirit Annie shared with her father. Greg had figured that out in five minutes. A jaunty towheaded tomboy greeted him from a framed Polaroid. All dressed up for her prom, a crooked corsage drooped over her left breast, a totally cowed boy slouched on her right.

Rusty leaned over to get a view of the kitchen, making sure they weren't overheard. "She could bull-doze any boy even then."

Or man, Greg thought with a wry smile. The fact that she hadn't gotten through to him yet only showed how thick his walls had become. Why was he so afraid of a second chance?

He followed Rusty's gaze and found himself watching a woman humming over a stove, sneaking a sip of red wine, fussing over tossed salads. While Rusty studied him, Greg fought the urge to stand up straighter, finger-comb his hair, remember what he paid for his last corsage. "She can take care of herself," he said out of nowhere.

Rusty nodded, his square jaw bobbing toward his chest. "I taught her to."

"Turns out your dad and I worked on a picture together."

Annie's eyes grew wide as she bounced a hot biscuit on her fingertips. "When?"

"When he was a cocky-as-they-come stuntman just starting out," Rusty answered. "Didn't recognize him at first."

Annie howled with laughter as Rusty recounted one hair-raising stunt after another. "Well, well, well."

She laughed. She plopped a huge dollop of mashed potatoes on Greg's plate, then skipped into the kitchen to get a jar of mustard. "For the original hot dog."

Greg burned good-naturedly. "Too many hormones, not enough sense. When you realize you're not immortal, you wise up."

"When you realize you're not immortal, you put everything you can into living," Annie countered.

"You plan for every contingency."

"You go with the flow."

Rusty looked from his daughter to the man seated opposite her. "How do you know which way it's flowing? Look at women doing men's jobs—"

"Daddy."

Her exasperated tone gave Greg the idea she'd heard this speech before.

"Now, I'm paying you a compliment here. Let me make my point. My daughter here is a perfect example of life never doing what you expect. You'd think she was raised to roughhouse all day, racing around this place on her pony. But she also learned to cook, shop, sew—"

"Only because Mom refused to make my barrel-riding outfits."

"I mean later. She did all that despite a mother who walked out on us, a brother who left us even quicker, a father who's all but useless lately—"

"Daddy." Annie gave his hand a squeeze.

"Sometimes I think she's living for all of us."

She cleared her throat and jumped up from the

table. "If you want to play "Father Knows Best," I'll play Donna Reed and clear the dishes."

"I think you embarrassed her," Greg said when they were alone.

Rusty shook his head. "She's a great rebounder, no matter what life hands her. She's never been afraid of anything. I encouraged that, though maybe I shouldn't have."

"Afraid she'll get hurt?"

The old man's jaw tightened. "After what this family's been through? What do you think?"

"I'm sorry."

He threw his napkin on the table, his voice firm enough to carry to the kitchen. "We're in this life to live it. We take our chances. If you love someone, you take those chances with 'em. Now if you'll excuse me, the ball game's on."

Greg heard the smile in Annie's voice before he turned.

"Believe it or not, I didn't write that speech for him." She opened the screen door with her shoulder and stepped onto the porch, handing him a lemonade.

He put his arm around her without giving it a second thought. It seemed the natural thing to do. "You know, I was thinking. We haven't been on many real dates."

"Do dinners at the cantina count?"

"You deserve better."

"Yes, I do."

He laughed. They sat together on the swing and watched the stars. The Angels announcer gave the score for the third inning as Rusty turned up the radio inside.

"Great guy," Greg murmured.

"Great guy."

"Proud of you."

"I'm proud of him. He kept us all together when Mom left. Made life into an adventure. He always supported me."

"Which I don't do."

"Which you could."

"You never need encouragement."

"Maybe I don't need so much protection either."

"Criticizing my management style?"

"Nope. I'm too full of stew to argue about anything right now."

Greg took that as an opening. He drew a line down her brow, his fingertip damp with perspiration from the glass. "What are you afraid of?"

"Not much."

"Annie?"

Her eyes raised to his. "I didn't know it showed."

"Something's bothering you. Tell me."

She leaned her head against his shoulder. Undefined doubts had crept up on her all evening. Putting them into words involved effort, risk. "Dad said something at dinner about how I've lived for all of us. I did everything I could to make up for Mom being gone, although I knew I'd never be her. I wanted to be Cody most of my life."

They both laughed.

"And I was, after he died. I competed and raced and took all the risks he would have taken. I wouldn't let myself be afraid. And then there were Dad's operations and the canes and the chair. He wouldn't let me pamper him, wanted me to get out and live. So I did. For all of us."

They listened to the evening sounds.

"Is that bad?" Greg asked.

"It is if I'm attracted to you because of what you've lost. Maybe I'm trying to make up for Pam too."

NINE

The idea stunned him. Greg set his lemonade on the porch, rocking the swing to a halt. "That'd be a big order to fill. Especially since you didn't know her."

"She could be Meryl Streep, Mother Theresa, and Jane Pauley rolled into one."

"She wasn't." Greg felt lower than a prairie dog's belly. So, she thought that was his problem. "I'm not holding back because I'm comparing the two of you. That isn't it, Annie."

"No?"

The small word, faintly asked, made him want to lash out. He'd been blind, selfish, and self-centered; so worried about his own pain he hadn't realized she had insecurities too; convinced he could take her flirting and flattery and owe her nothing in return. "Meeting your father made me see some things. How backward this whole relationship has been from the start."

"This is the twentieth century, Greg. Women pursue men if they want."

"Yeah. You tease me—"

"You yell at me."

"You throw me around."

"Or climb all over you."

The heat started, instant and insatiable. "You crawl into my bed."

"Hush. I didn't mean to do that."

For all her bravado, Annie hadn't forgotten Rusty was only a wall away. "Afraid your father will hear?"

"You should be. He can be an ornery cuss, especially when I bring someone home."

"Let him chase me off the ranch, I probably deserve it."

"Why?"

He touched her neck, drawing an invisible boundary from her earlobe to her collar. "For not telling you the kind of things a man tells a woman he's attracted to."

He told her every time he called her Silk, Annie thought, every time he looked at her with that hungry look. "Such as?"

"Maybe I won't know until I try."

That's all she'd ever wanted to hear—that he'd give them a chance. She folded her arms, noting the chills chasing up her spine. Anxiety linked with fear until they were nearly indistinguishable. But Annie never gave in to something as useless as fear or as flimsy as hope. A woman could brazen out any situation if she kept up her nerve. He was attracted to her. The least she could do was hear him out, even if his next sentence was, "I like you but—"

She tilted her chin at the sauciest possible angle she could manage and looked him in the eye. "Well?"

"I'm feeling things I didn't think I'd ever feel again. Struggling."

She heard it in his earnest tone, the searching pauses between his words. "Loving means letting someone in. It's not something you forget."

"You mean Pam."

"You married her."

"I loved her." He meant that. He couldn't explain how the love, the memory of it, had changed in the last few weeks. "It sounds stupid, but it's similar to an injured muscle, it hurts when you use it again."

"It has to feel good to know it's still there."

"Yeah. But you've gotta wonder if it'll ever be the same."

"Does it have to be? I can't be her."

He crooked a knowing smile, trying to get that worry out of her eyes. "You aren't. You sass me and boss me and never ever let me forget you've got a mind of your own."

"You got that right."

"See what I mean? Heck, I'll probably never live this down, but I even admire the way you stand up to me."

"You do?"

"It drives me nuts, but yeah. You've got more guts than half the guys I work with."

A woman presented with a bouquet of roses couldn't have looked more demurely pleased. "Why, thank you."

Greg shifted on the seat and tried another one. "I like the way you've won over the crew too."

She nodded at their joined hands, then lifted her gaze to his. "And the way I've won you over?"

He couldn't resist the dare hidden there, or the vulnerability. "The way you've tried."

Her gaze faltered. He went back to feeling like a scoundrel, an uncomfortably familiar feeling. All he'd meant was he admired her courage. She'd kept after him, pestering him, not letting him retreat into that shell he'd hidden in for five years. She kept dragging him out into the light of day and burrowing into his dreams. *I don't know what I can give you, Annie. I want it to be enough. To be right.* "I'm lousy at this. I sound like some cowpoke fresh off the ranch trying to sweet-talk a lady."

At least the hurt in her eyes vanished when she laughed at him. "You could give my father lessons in crusty-but-lovable."

"I never was good at love talk."

"You manage in other ways."

"Yeah?"

She nodded solemnly, her teeth biting into her lower lip.

He didn't need more encouragement. Around Annie he needed one perky step, one spunky dare, one yearning look, and he was ready to haul her into his arms. Was that love? It was so different from what he'd had with Pam. So all-fired similar. Keeping her close mattered. Making her his meant everything.

Words didn't count when her mouth parted slightly, her breath skimming his. Their lips touched. He broke away, briefly, letting no more than a whisper part them while he gazed one more time at her sleepy eyes. In the shadow he cast, her irises grew wide and dark. "You're the sexiest woman I've known, Annie."

"I know," she retorted, impertinent, game. "Are you going to kiss me or talk to me about it?"

He kissed her. Eyes open this time.

They said it best without words, communicating need with desire, wants without hesitation.

She curled one arm under his. He inhaled deeply, knowing she'd feel the stretch of muscle across his back, wanting her to feel the strength surging through him—strength she'd put there. Her other hand strafed the taut cords of his neck, making his body tighten everywhere, a hot rush suffusing his skin.

Wanting Annie took on added urgency. His heart had hardened into crevices he'd never expected to heal. Feelings filled him when she touched him, like flood-waters filling gullies, breaking down clumps of earth and melting them together, making them whole again. He hadn't been able to say it, but if healing meant hurting, he wanted all the hurt she had. "Annie."

"Greg."

Her body strained toward his. He wanted to let her show him the way, but the pulsing commands in his blood shook off restraint. He squeezed her until she moaned for breath. His fingers threaded through her hair, cradling her head, holding it close. He filled her mouth with his tongue, parrying her tantalizing forays with thrusts of his own.

He'd be inside her in every way. He'd show her what he couldn't say, things he wasn't even sure of until he held her in his arms. If he could ever love again, Annie was the woman.

His hand trespassed between her knees, catching the heat collected where her jeans touched.

"You two going to bed soon?"

They broke apart like teenagers after curfew, jumping to their feet. Greg cussed, bending to pick up the lemonade he'd kicked over.

Her father peered out from behind the screen door. "Can't hear me coming on these rubber wheels," Rusty cackled.

"Lucky you weren't in that thing when I was in high school," Annie snapped, "you would've scared my boyfriends out of a year's growth!"

"Have her tell you about some of those bozos sometime. And don't forget to turn out the lights before you two turn in."

"Right," she muttered as her father rolled away.

For a woman who only wore her hair one way, long and straight and pulled off her face, Annie found a dozen ways to fuss with it now. She tucked a strand behind her ear, then untucked it. She blew a wisp off her cheek. "Guess we ought to be heading upstairs."

"Okay."

Annie peered at him. Her heart thudded painfully. She didn't know if it was due to the aftershock of her father's sudden bark or to Greg's softly suggestive reply. She'd been about to go further than prudent. Not that prudence ranked high in Annie's approach to life. But love and stunt work had a lot in common. A woman needed to trust the person she worked with. She sure as shootin' had to know what she was headed for. In Greg's arms, on a swing still swaying from their hasty exit, she'd been about to do something incredibly risky without so much as a hint as to where it led.

"Your room is at the top of the stairs," she said, just in case he'd misunderstood.

"And his?"

"Ground floor. And don't get any ideas."

She swung open the screen. Greg pressed a palm flat against it. He pinned her body between his and the house. "What I've got are more like fantasies."

Maybe they were, Annie thought, scanning his eyes for some sign. Maybe loving him was the biggest fantasy of all. He'd come right out and said he might never return her love.

Would she jump off a ledge without a net? Run into a burning building without knowing the exits? *Make love in the backseat of a car racing down a mountainside?*

She'd come through it all right because Greg had been there.

And because you bailed out in time, her conscience reminded her. Maybe that was the wisest course of action.

He tilted her chin in his direction, a bemused smile slanting across his face. "My Annie nervous?"

It wasn't bedroom jitters making her seek everywhere but his eyes. One person could mark your life forever, like a brand or a scar. It wasn't always a matter of getting to your feet and starting over. Who knew that better than Greg?

"Tell me what's wrong," he demanded, his hoarse voice catching.

She gave him that much. Then a little more. "I think I love you, as much as you don't want me to. Taking another foolish risk without your permission, I guess." Her words subsided to a whisper. "I don't know if I can take the next risk alone."

He ran a hand through his hair, then flattened both palms on either side of her. Like Sisyphus sentenced to roll a boulder up a hill for eternity, Greg pushed at the weight in his heart. Every time he thought it was gone, it rolled back. "I don't know either, Annie. I don't know what I can feel. Maybe it isn't in me to love a woman the way I used to."

Her smile was sad and fleeting. "In that case, I'm not sure I'm that brave."

He looked at her a long time. The words didn't come. What more could he say? He was willing to try, dammit. But guarantees . . .

"Good night, Greg."

If she felt his frustrated gaze on her back all the way to the foot of the stairs, she didn't show it. He stood there listening until she reached the top. She flicked on the light to his room. Then she fled down the hall. The lock on her bedroom door clicked like a cocked trigger pointed at his heart.

All the nerve in the world and it had to fail her now! Half-dressed, Annie paced in her room. She'd started tossing off clothes the moment the door slammed behind her. She sat on her bed, but couldn't stay.

She looked out at the desert, a razor-straight road leading off the ranch to the highway, the beams of a distant semi passing by. She was home. She'd come because she felt safe there.

It was her refuge, a place to lick her wounds, physical and emotional, to recharge. When Greg touched her, she felt more charged than a double-D battery. If she let him love her, what would the consequences be? If he loved her there, where would she go in the whole wide world to forget him?

Shoving her fists in the arms of a flannel shirt, Annie dug through a drawer for khaki pants. She'd go for a walk while the moon rose. If she couldn't outthink her fears, she'd outwork them. Physical exertion cleared the cobwebs. If she pictured her fears, she could defeat them. Pterodactyls, dinosaurs, bears, dragons—

How did a woman defeat the man she loved? How

could she slay the dragon inside him? "Especially when he's in love with it."

Annie winced; that wasn't right. Pam wasn't the villain. There were no villains. Greg had loved his wife, heart and soul. Was it right to ask him to love her instead? Could she compete with a ghost?

She'd been competing with them all her life. Her mother, Cody, Rusty's youth. All the things she'd made up for with her own fire and zest for living. Her enthusiasm and spark had filled up a lot of empty spaces. Was she trying to fill up Pam's absence?

If she'd made up in some small way for the losses her family had sustained, she'd never regretted it for an instant. But she wanted to mean more to Greg than a substitute. Much more. If he couldn't see that, what could she do?

A noise outside drew her to the window. He stood on the porch, smoke from a rare cigarette curling upward. He only smoked before a stunt or when he was troubled; she knew him that well. He tried so hard to conceal his emotions, to protect them. "You don't have to protect yourself from me."

She'd been in love before, but never like this. Each man had been an equal, a free spirit like herself, each able to walk away after a frank good-bye.

Greg was different. She'd concentrated so much on his feelings, she wasn't sure of hers. She'd watched him come alive, irritated as a bear awakened from hibernation, yet eager to live, sexually charged, revived. She'd taken the credit for all of it, never realizing until now that giving was easy. Taking meant being vulnerable, letting someone in. Suddenly the risks were all hers.

It wasn't fair, it wasn't equal, there were no guarantees. "Live life as it is, not as it ought to be." Easier said than done.

She took off the flannel shirt, running her hands across the back of the chair as if it were the yoke of his shoulders. On the porch below he stilled. She wondered if he felt that. Her breath frosted the pane. She reluctantly drew back.

Unzipping the khaki slacks, she let them drop. A gauzy chiffon nightgown whispered across her skin. Pacing all night would keep Dad awake. Better to get in bed, stare at the stars, and try to sleep. Maybe the dragon would come to her in a dream and she'd figure out a way to slay it without hurting the man it guarded.

Greg stopped at the bottom of the wheelchair ramp, grinding his half-smoked cigarette in the dirt. He ambled into the desert; any direction would do. He'd go out and join the coyotes in one long lonely howl at the moon.

What had he said wrong? That he wasn't sure he could love her? Not much of a proposition for a woman to stake her body on.

Pam would've sent him packing.

But he'd never expected Annie to run from anything, including him.

What had Rusty said at dinner? *"You take your chances. If you love someone, you take the chances with 'em."* Sure, it had Wise Old Coot written all over it. Beneath it was a father who cared about his daughter and wanted Greg to give her a chance. Could he?

Greg looked over his shoulder at the square of light in an upper window, growing smaller the farther he walked from the house. "I care about her too, old man." She'd gotten inside that rock he called a heart. But was it love? Was it enough?

Pebbles crunched beneath his boots, the ground more sand than soil. The air whistled by him, brisk and sharp with sage. Brittle vegetation crackled underfoot. Nocturnal animals scurried as his heels scuffed the desert floor. Pam always said he clammed up when he thought things out. Not this time. He had to talk to someone, and Annie had locked him out. In more ways than one.

He craned his neck, squinting at the remote glittering stars. His fists hung loose at his sides. His body ached, unused, unshared.

"What do I do, Pam? She asked me if I still loved you. That's what's bothering her, I know it. Hell, it bothers me. I loved you. Maybe I still do. Does that mean I'm supposed to stop living?"

He felt like a fool, talking to thin air. That didn't stop him from getting down on one knee, digging up a fistful of sand, and letting it sift through his clenched fist. "Dammit, Pam. I loved you so much, I didn't think I'd ever feel anything again. But is this what you want? You want me to be alone forever?"

He listened to his voice die in the dark. What was the sense in carping at her? He already knew the answer. She'd never have wanted him to live alone. She loved him. She'd have wanted him to be happy.

Not that she'd ever said it. They'd never talked about a future without each other, never considered it. There were a lot of things they'd never gotten around to.

And never would.

"I can't forget you. But I want to try again. I don't feel as if I'm cheating on you. I just want to know it's okay. Could you tell me that?"

He stood, ramming both his fists in his pockets. He let out a gust of air. This was nuts, standing around waiting for some kind of sign.

A rustling sound brushed the ground behind him. Greg wheeled, expecting a coyote, a stray cat from one of the barns. A woman in gauzy white drifted toward him, her hair ivory in the moonlight. Her gown wafting around her ankles, her feet hidden, she seemed to float.

Greg swallowed the heart that leapt into his throat. "Annie."

She didn't answer.

He huffed out another sigh and planted his hands on his hips. "Are you sleepwalking again?"

Her silence was like a precious reprieve. He could watch her and she'd never know, her hair swirling in the air around her, her expression dreamy and ethereal. The womanly body inside the filmy cloth was more substantial than the blank gaze.

She continued toward him as if drawn by his voice,

pausing a few feet away. "Where is he?" she asked anxiously.

"You looking for Cody?"

She didn't say.

Greg knew the answer. She'd come looking for him. He cocked his head toward the sky. If Pam was laughing, he didn't hear it. His own rueful laugh jarred the night. "You sure know how to give a man a sign."

Agitated, Annie turned. Greg reminded himself he shouldn't wake her, but he couldn't let her wander off. "Did your dad ever find you out here in the mornings or do you only do this for my benefit?"

He didn't really expect an answer. He noticed her bare feet again. "You could hurt yourself walking around without shoes, step on a snake, a bottle top, a nail." Stub her precious toe.

At least Annie slept while sleepwalking. What was his excuse? The fact that he worried about her constantly should have told him how much he cared. From the start he'd treated Julie McLean like another professional. Not Annie.

Not that she'd treated him any more professionally. With Annie everything was personal. She danced by him, flirting, challenging, never letting him forget he was still a man. She'd reminded him how it felt to be alive, to yearn, to covet, even lust. Especially lust.

If he could wrap up his feelings and call them gratitude, he'd thank her for her efforts and be on his way. But they went deeper than that, right past the scars and hurt and into a corner of his heart he hadn't used in years—one Pam had left behind, a buried treasure for another woman to find.

Annie moved away, tugging to be free. Irritated, distressed, she batted his hand away. "He's here. I know it."

He stepped in front of her, purposely letting her bump his chest and feel the real man. "He's here, Annie. Right in front of you. I'm sorry he gave you such a hard time."

She darted her head left and right as if listening to a sound far off. She began walking again.

He let her steer them toward the house, his toes gripping inside his boots every time she put her foot down. He couldn't stand it. The risk of waking her paled against the risk of her stomping on something sharp. "Hang on, darlin'. The midnight stroll is over." He swept her into his arms.

She didn't struggle. Accepting his touch, she let her body ease into his. He tried to ignore the bounce of her hips against his lower abdomen, the growing evidence of need. He'd thought himself too aggravated to get aroused. *Yeah, and four weeks ago you thought you'd never love another woman again.* He was about to. If she'd let him.

He directed her arms around his neck. She complied. Her apprehensive look stayed. "It's okay," he murmured more times than strictly necessary. They crossed a hundred yards of empty desert, heading toward the house. "I'm taking you to bed."

His steps slowed. Between there and her home he

had a lot of explaining to do. Since she couldn't tell him how she felt, he'd tell her. "Maybe you can't hear me. Maybe this is a coward's way out, but you've been chasing me from the start. Somehow I got the idea this was easy for you.

"But sleepwalking means you're worried and I'm the reason. If I haven't said what I should, it's because I wasn't sure I could live up to any promises, and, honey, I'd promise you just about anything." A few more steps. A few more stars winking. "I want to be honest. I want to take the chance. But I hate the idea it's you who has to chance it with me."

As he walked, the words came easier. Things he hadn't thought he could say emerged one after the other. How he'd wanted her, missed her when she wasn't around. How the very strength of his feelings had kept him from naming them. How everything he'd tried to say on the porch earlier was true.

"You know that swishy way you walk? As if you're in a hurry but no hurry's going to get in the way of you enjoying yourself on the way there? I love that." And the stunts. "I know what you mean about the thrills, the way they put life in perspective. We may not heal people or cure diseases, but we can show them some excitement. Maybe it's all fantasy, but we make it come true. You showed me, Annie."

On the edge of the compound they passed beneath the spiky shadow cast by the windmill. An old back injury began to throb. "Speaking of stunts—" Greg paused at the first bunkhouse they came to, the one farthest from the house. He set her on her feet on the wide weathered planks of the porch.

He'd been about to say, "Give me a second to rest." The words never made it past his lips. She swayed into him, her arms still around his neck, her breasts pressed lightly to his chest. He brushed a kiss across her chin.

"Give me another chance." The top of her thigh brushed the bulge in his jeans. The words dried up. Fierce bounding flames took their place. "Annie."

He stepped in closer, feeling her breasts through her gauze and his flannel. Holding her slender waist in his hands, then one splendid breast in his palm, he cherished her for a moment.

Her eyes closed, her mouth turned up at the corners, dreaming of something sultry, pleasing, too private for him to see. It wasn't right, touching her like this.

"This isn't a dream." His thumb scraped across her nipple, urging it to a peak. His eyes narrowed on her face for any sign she felt that, any sign at all. He pleasured her twice more, a little rougher each time. "This is real. Make it real with me."

She sighed and went still. He got up on the step with her, his feet planted on either side of hers. He slanted his hips forward in small pulsing movements, torturing himself with the taste of something he could have if only—

He closed his eyes, skimming his hands down her back, molding her to him. He inhaled the scent of her hair. "Annie, Annie. Wake up," he breathed. "We've both been asleep too long."

Her hands moved. He froze, waiting. "Touch me, Annie. Touch me back."

She did it because he asked her to, because they were the first words she heard as she awoke. Surfacing from a deep, disturbing dream, Annie didn't know how long she'd been awake or how real anything was. He'd haunted her dreams for so long. Why should tonight be any different?

Her palms rasped against the denim of his faded jeans, intimate as whispers in the dark. She felt the muscles bunch, his thighs firm and warm.

She detected the roughened skin of his fingertips drawing her gown up, pausing above her knees, then rising, gingerly skimming the golden hair on her thighs. She felt her knees buckle.

Her body was on fire. His nearness added to the heat. His breathing came hard. One of his hands splayed on her thigh, a thumb straying awkwardly toward the junction. Trembling from head to toe, she knew he'd find moistness there.

"Sh," he murmured, sensing her tension, sheltering her body with his. He let her gown drop, folding her in his arms as if the crisp night air caused her quaking. The gesture could have been protective. It was far from innocent. Aroused, he pressed against her with all the arrogant pride a man possessed. He clearly wanted her to feel it, even if she wouldn't remember a thing in the morning. "I'll take you home in a minute."

"Take me home now."

He halted, his arms around her. "Annie?"

"It isn't your fault. I'm sorry–" She pushed him away. He stayed right where he was. Moonlight hardened the planes of his face, casting him in shadows of cool silver and black velvet. He left it up to her to step out of his arms.

"You know this isn't right," she said, "touching someone without their permission."

"I love touching you. I've done it before."

"When I was awake."

"You're awake now." He nudged her cheek, dropping kisses on her jaw. "You're not traumatized, are you?"

"This is no time for teasing." She shoved him away. He staggered off the step, more surprised than anything. He came right back, joining her on the platform, and his body suddenly seemed too large and solid to share this space with her. "It's very disturbing waking up like this."

"With a man you don't know?"

"I know you, all right. That's why it's disturbing."

His chuckle died. He hadn't thought the woman could get any paler in the moonlight. "I was about to take you back. Honest. I just wanted—"

"I'll bet you did!" She crossed her arms, uncrossed them, clenched her fists at her sides, then folded them into her bent elbows.

"I wanted to show you—"

"What?"

He worked his jaw. "For the last few weeks I've been showing you what I want physically. I wanted to show you how I felt."

Annie confined her agitation to curling her toes on the dry boards. Deflecting him with sarcasm seemed her only protection. "You have feelings? This is the first I've heard of them."

"I tried to tell you tonight."

"On the porch."

"And a minute ago."

"When I couldn't hear."

"I didn't know how you'd take it."

"But you planned on giving it to me." She stormed off.

He gripped her arm, spinning her toward him. "I don't deserve that. You know how it is the minute we get close to each other. That doesn't change at night, Annie."

"Or when I'm asleep?"

"Not ever. I want you, Annie. Everything you can give."

Isolation surrounded them. They were a hundred feet from the house, outside the tiniest one-room bunkhouse on the ranch. The yard light threw their shadows against the clapboards. In the distance a coyote chose the moment to howl. "And what will you give me?"

His voice rasped like the rusted windmill. "Everything I can." He took her hand and urged her onto the porch with him. "I've felt it since the first time I touched you in the backseat of that car. Don't argue. Don't say it's only lust. We've got something. We can work on the rest. Give it a chance. Give us a chance." He trailed a kiss along the swell of her shoulder.

Heaven help her, she let him.

"I'm sorry if I scared you, Annie. Sorry I upset you so much, you came sleepwalking out here."

Sensations as faint as heat lightning shimmered on her skin. Her heart beat like thunder beyond the horizon. Half the night lay before them.

"I'm glad you came looking for me, Annie."

Yes. She had.

"Touch me again."

TEN

Up until this moment, Annie had overcome all her fears herself. She'd thought that's what courage was. Maybe love meant asking someone to share your fears. "I'm going to need help with this."

"That nightgown can't have that many buttons."

She laughed, a short breathless sound. Teasing wasn't the kind of help she had in mind. But it worked, easing her some, giving her courage. "I'm not expecting promises."

"You mean I can't promise you the greatest, hottest sex you've had in your life?"

She raised a brow, apparently unimpressed. "That good, huh?"

He crooked a finger under her chin and lifted it an inch higher. "You doubt it?"

Her body responded instantly. The touch of one finger made her quiver. She'd seen him violent with passion; she'd seen him resist. No man, no stunt, no danger, ever made her feel more alive. She'd never be asked to lay more on the line—matching passion for passion, the rough with the soft, the tender with the ferocious, placing one willing, untested heart up against a scarred and cautious one.

He misunderstood her silence. He paced on the narrow porch. "We do this because we're both ready and we both want it. Or we don't do it at all."

His concern made her smile; it always had. "Walking me through it, boss?"

"I want to know you're with me all the way, Annie. Do you want this?"

"Do I want *you*?" She touched the crescent scar on his cheek. *Live it now*, her heart whispered. Who knew what could happen tomorrow?

Her gaze flickered to the house and back. When he turned to look, her fingers grazed his lips. He closed his eyes as if tasting nectar. "Annie."

Courage surged through her, the absolute necessity of living now, taking everything life gave, even the flawed tentative stirrings of a man's injured heart. When the chances were slim, one concentrated that much harder. When the stunt was dangerous, one never even considered failure. "I think we need some privacy."

He reached around her, tugging at the bunkhouse's screen door. He used his shoulder on the warped door inside, giving it a discreet shove. They entered, her body brushing him as he held the door.

Long unused, the room was bare of everything save a plain wooden chair painted white and a single twin bed. Moonlight cast a white rectangle on the bed, a distorted image of the only window. Greg stayed in the doorway, letting her get her bearings. There wasn't much to see.

"Dad reserves this one for the foreman when he hires temporary crews."

"If you're not sure, Annie, tell me and I'll leave."

Chilled, she sat on a mattress covered with a faded flower sheet, a scratchy dark green blanket folded at the foot. She owed him the one thing he'd always demanded of her, gut-check honesty. "I'm not sure."

He caught hold of the door as it creaked, his fist tight on the handle. "Then maybe I'd better go."

She called softly after him. "I don't want you to do that either."

His groan made her smile. "All the times I've touched you—it never involved so much talk before."

She was falling fast. She'd have to put her trust in fate to land her on her feet. She tried a sultry pose, leaning back on the bed, one leg crossed over the other, her toe nervously tapping in the moonlight. "Then come on over here, Mr. Ford."

He stepped close. She fought the urge to rest her hand on his leg. It would be so easy to reach up and stroke the ridged muscle beneath the denim. She ground her palms into the mattress instead. The musty cabin air tickled her lungs. "Who's hesitating now?" she teased.

"I want to be sure we both know what we're getting into."

"A lot of trouble and a narrow bed."

"Annie."

"Sorry. No more kidding."

Neither voice rose above a murmur. Offers were tendered, the erratic, uncertain, reluctant beginnings of love.

"You do that when you're scared," he said.

"Tease you? I do that when I'm trying to stop you from worrying. I can't undo your past, Greg. But I can give you one hell of a present."

He stroked her cheek. "A gift from the angels?"

A wry smile saved her. "Now don't go getting all romantic on me. I wouldn't know how to take it." She shook out her hair, letting it whisper across her back. *Everything*, she promised him silently. "Don't let the doubts hold you back."

"I'm afraid of hurting you."

"We can't predict what will happen."

"I meant now. Here." He bent to kiss her, skimming the hair off her neck. His teeth nipped, gentle, sharp.

She gasped, a stuttering half breath, part shock, part desire. "Greg."

"We've been there before, but something's always stopped us. What's to stop us now, Annie? What will protect you from me?"

She sensed his greater strength, intensely aware of their isolation. It wasn't his size that cautioned her, but the roiling tension that took every ounce of his self-control to contain. He kept it in check for her sake.

Fear him? She loved him even more. He was tough as mesa sandstone with a heart as big as all outdoors. She could make her own place in that heart, giving him things Pam never had. Strength, daring, defiance.

Compliance. She angled her arms around his neck, swaying in a slow dance, an intimate tango of hips brushing hips. She kissed the unsteady pulse hidden in the hollow at the base of his throat. She scraped her sensitive mouth over the stubble where his throat met the shadowed underside of his clenched jaw. She sought out the tautly corded side of his neck. And bit him back.

His grip crushed fistfuls of her gown. "I don't want to hurt you."

"Passion gets out of hand," she panted, "or it isn't passion."

"I can take it slow."

"And I can take it, Greg. Anything."

His sassy Annie. She swayed her hips back and forth against the front of his jeans and did a dip that parted her knees, fitting his leg snugly between hers. She kissed his throat again. His Adam's apple felt like one tight knot. He swallowed and swallowed again.

"You need me," she said.

His rigid posture clashed with the feathery touch of his fingers against her face. His hand shook.

"You need a woman, not a ghost, not a memory." Her lips brushed his.

He broke, scouring her with kisses no suave Romeo would dare, stark, brutal, hungry, stricken. He was tired of control, of outthinking whatever life might throw at him. "Let's do it."

He embraced her until she thought she'd faint from lack of air. He opened his mouth to her and she was lost, drowning in the desert.

Annie knew the real thing when it hit her. Like a tornado sweeping her off her feet, love was messy, passionate, real. The right words didn't always get said. Candles didn't light and moody music didn't play in the background. The outskirts of the ranch were desolate, the night air cold. The cabin was grimy, the sheets musty and stiff.

She didn't give a damn. For once, he bared his soul to her in the hunger of his body, his loneliness in a possessive touch. He wanted *her*. She felt like crying for joy. "Love me," she whispered.

"I do."

They had the moon for light and the stars for witnesses.

He swung her around until the backs of her legs hit the edge of the bed. It wasn't gentle or cautious. He shoved her gown up her knees and showed her how to wrap her legs around him. He kissed her neck, the silvery slope of a bared shoulder. He wanted to kiss her breasts, but her gown got in the way. "If you don't take this thing off, I can't guarantee it'll stay in one piece."

The threat beneath the warning made her shiver. "It's all I have on."

"So I noticed." He spoke through clenched teeth, second-guessing himself one last time. She hadn't exactly said no.

The neckline ended between her breasts, an unbuttoned V. He grasped it with his fists. One sharp tear split the fabric to her waist. Air rushed against her bare skin, followed by his breath, his touch. Before she could speak, he took a peaked nipple into his mouth. She tensed, a small cry. Did she think he would hurt her? Had he?

He rested his forehead against her abdomen, his eyes clenched tight. The pause did little to restore his control. The aroma of her skin filled him, the scent of her heat. Shreds of her gown taunted him. "Annie."

"No." She leaned back, balanced on both hands, arching into him. "Don't stop."

"We've got to." He unceremoniously unhooked her legs from around his waist. He stood, his boot heels scuffing the floor as he turned one way, then the next, a hand clamped to the back of his neck. "What the hell am I doing here?"

He didn't miss the way her breath caught nor the slight shake in her voice. "Loving me?"

He felt mean, wrought up, as coiled as a spring with no way to unwind. The last thing he wanted to do was take this out on her. "You call this love? I'm practically attacking you. I should be—nicer."

She scrunched up her face. *"Nicer?"*

He winced, then scowled. He was messing this up but good. "A man should be careful with a woman he loves. Gentle, considerate, patient. Everybody knows that." It was practically written in a script, the one he carried around inside him.

"Like Pam?" she asked.

The words hit him hard. He stared into those unblinking eyes of hers, that gaze she pinned him with when he was going around the bend obsessing over details. "A careful man—"

"A careful man is still a man. You think you have to love me the way you loved her?"

He dragged both hands through his hair. He'd yank the words out of his scalp if he had to. "I didn't say that. This is new to me, Annie."

"It's as old as men and women."

Maybe it was. Maybe what he'd had with Pam had been the new part. She'd taken a rough-and-tumble cowboy and made him tender, made him take his time, taught him how she needed to be loved. Annie was different. What she brought out in him went as far back as caveman days. It spoke to something deep inside him, dark, dangerous, and unbridled. Something modern women weren't supposed to want. To call it uncivilized understated it by a mile. To call it sex didn't even begin to encompass it. He wanted to make her his in the most primitive, protective, permanent way possible. He wanted to love her until neither one of them could walk straight.

Annie stood up. For a moment he thought she swayed, but that was the slow sashay of a woman's walk, a woman who knew what she wanted. Stopping before him, raising her chin to look him in the eye, she licked the tip of her index finger, luxuriantly, as if it were an ice cream cone. Then she touched its damp tip to the scar on his chin. Pushing softly, she said, "You've walked me through it enough, boss. I think I'm ready."

Something expanded inside him, something that said it was okay. That something spoke in Annie's voice. His hands felt cumbersome, clumsy, his voice grating in the dark. "Anytime you want to stop, say so."

"Don't stop." She whispered it against his neck, her breath hot as the desert, humid as any jungle.

"Annie?"

"Don't stop," she murmured. She'd gotten through to him and she knew it. She would've kept right on kissing him if he hadn't held her back.

"We might have to." Hell, she'd probably slug him, but he had to say it. "I need some help getting these boots off."

"You what?"

The words fell between them with the force of a two-ton weight.

"I never wear 'em to bed."

"I should hope not."

"I broke both my ankles in that stock car picture when I spun out—"

"—at a hundred and ten miles an hour. Don't tell me." He'd entertained her one night in the cantina with one near-miss anecdote after another. She didn't find them funny anymore. She gestured toward the bed. "Go on. Sit down."

The bed creaked like nails down a chalkboard. His shoulder blades hit the wall, knocking a yellowed old calendar aslant. He stuck his foot straight out, as ordered. "The tighter the boots, the better the ankle support."

"Right." She cupped his heel with one hand and his calf with the other. "How do you get these off when you're alone?"

"Carefully. Ow."

She stopped dead, fixing him with a level look. "Don't tell me you're a big baby about pain."

"I'm not going to pretend I enjoy it. I'm not the Marquis de Sade, you know."

"Lucky me."

"Just don't twist it to the left."

"All right. On three. One. Two. Three." Annie yanked. Nothing. She switched her hair around to the other side, a silvery cascade baring the nape of her neck.

The desire to strafe that innocent skin with lewd kisses almost made him forget the boots.

Her rear end indelicately pushed his way, she balanced his foot on her thigh and wrapped her arms around the boot again. "You know, there's absolutely no way to do this romantically," she observed.

"Oh, I don't know about that."

She shot him another look. "One. Two. Ugh. You could help, you know."

He shrugged and lifted his other boot. "If you say so."

"You touch that toe to my behind and you're horse-meat, Ford. I'll do it myself." She gave the strangled boot another yank. Not an inch.

While her hands were busy elsewhere, Greg leaned forward. He petted her sweet behind with one hand. She swatted at him. He cupped her with both.

She jerked upright and swung around. "Stop that."

His heel hit the floor. He leaned back again, his shoulders in a "who, me?" shrug, his chest hollowed, his abdomen flatter than roadkill. "Anything you say, sugar." He waggled his outstretched foot once more.

Squinting in her best imitation of him in a bad mood, Annie stepped over his leg and planted her feet on either side. With his knee pinned between both of hers, she placed one hand under the heel and the other on the sole. "One. Two. Three!"

With a whoosh the boot came off. The leg jerked up. Annie trapped it between her clenched thighs. "You're lucky I've got lightning reflexes."

"And great thighs." Greg moved his leg between hers, sending off rockets of sensation. "Want to do the other one?"

She gave him a quelling glare and stepped over his other leg with all the respect she'd give an electrified fence rail. "You're enjoying this."

"I wouldn't be a man if I wasn't."

"An infuriating one," she mumbled. "Now help me on this."

There wasn't a whole lot to do. He pointed his toe when she pulled, listening to her grunt. Maneuvering onto his side, he curved himself in a half circle, propped on an elbow. He touched her again and heard her breath catch in a completely different way. He grazed his free hand up her flank, bringing the nightgown with it. "You've got a beautiful body."

Her thighs clenched on either side of his calf. "Years of aerobics will do that to you."

"Ain't nothin' like what I'm going to do to you."

It had been funny up to now, Annie thought, jerking on the hand-tooled cowboy boot with every ounce of know-how she had. Unveiling a softly rounded cheek to the night air, he filled a dimple with his thumb. She moaned, she wriggled. He knew he had her trapped. He drew a finger along her honey-warm core. Suddenly, unexpectedly, she felt him kiss a pale expanse of skin.

With one mighty yank, the boot came off. The motion sent her staggering across the room, the stiff leather flapping in her hand. "Got it!"

Stockinged feet made him silent as a shadow as he came after her. He backed her all the way to the wall, easing his arms around her. "Face to face is even better," he murmured. His mouth closed over hers, stealing all hope she ever had of breathing again.

The boot hit the floor with a thud. They hardly noticed.

He slid his hands down her body, cupping her again

to lift her to him. "I'm the biggest risk you'll ever take and you know it."

He knew she couldn't resist a dare. His fingers fumbled with his zipper. A belt hissed out of its loopholes, the buckle clinking against the floor, its tongue wagging.

Before Annie could slide the jeans over his lean hips, Greg put a hand back for his wallet. "We're going to need this."

She watched him tear the foil packet with his teeth. Then he indicated his shirt, his last piece of clothing. "Think you can unbutton this? The way I'm feeling, I'd probably rip it."

"That'd make us even." She toyed with the shredded edges of her nightgown, her fingertips gliding low between her breasts. She rubbed the hem of his cotton shirt between her thumb and fingers, grazing the taut skin behind it. One button, two, up and up. She spread the shirt open, her palms flattening against his bare chest. When she kissed one nipple, his muscles clenched in a spasm of desire.

Two bodies wrestled, wrangled. They found their way to the mattress. Like Greg, it had very little give. Like the past, it didn't matter now.

He wanted this at her pace; he tried. Perspiration glistened on his torso. Her tongue darted out to taste it. What she did next would have reduced the world's best gentleman to a ruthless savage. "You're making me crazy," he breathed.

An inarticulate moan was no argument.

"Annie."

"You promised me everything. Love me. *Live* with me."

His last shred of control shook in his arms as he held himself off her. He'd done that once in the back-seat of a car, more gentleman than he gave himself credit for. But this was no place for restraint. This was the complete honesty people called love, the willing-ness to go the limit, to find the one person who could take you there, up to the very edge—and over it.

Annie arched herself to him, flesh glancing off flesh. She slipped her hand between them, guiding him in, welcoming him. "Dance with me."

His control broke. He kissed her once more. A rivulet of sweat raced from his temple and fell, tasting tangy on her lips. With one shattering thrust he plunged into her, swallowing her cry.

When it was over, they lay together breathing hard. They said nothing. Startling zigzags of sensation rippled beneath Annie's skin. They'd finished minutes ago. It was over. And yet something whispered to her heart that this was just the beginning.

ELEVEN

He caught her staring at the ceiling and kissed her eyes closed. His hand ranged over her body. She'd never felt so naked. The blanket lay tousled at the foot of the bed. She knew the feeling. Her smooth surface had been ruffled beyond all recognition, her neat edges mussed.

His lovemaking had been ruthless. Not cruel, but predatory, possessive. He'd sent her diving to the bottom of her soul and back again, making her wild with need, meeting it every time, taking her farther and farther until she had to trust him because he was all there was.

Minutes later memories seared her, a scalding kiss, an intimate touch so deep, so knowing, she'd gasped and begged for more. He'd seized on her passion, ravishing her with unbridled hunger. "Now, Annie, now." She wrapped her legs around him, high on his waist, giving her body to him utterly. "Annie!"

An ancient window curtain billowed over her head. She'd clutched it until it ripped, the fragile papery cloth rent in one long tear, broken threads dusting them like powdered stars.

Talk about living! Every inch of her hummed. Time couldn't lessen the brand of his touch, the shuddering aftereffect of their coming together. He nuzzled her arm with his nose, following that with kisses, a mild bite. She tried to catch her breath. Impossible. With her eyes closed, his nearness was too intense.

"Don't," she asked softly.

"I enjoy looking at you."

Her eyes searched his with a curiosity verging on worry. "You looked at me the night I came to your bed."

"We didn't do this then." He laughed, smoothing his fingers over her abdomen.

"I don't think anyone could sleepwalk through that."

"Uh-uh." He kissed her lips, a feathery near miss. She wasn't ready for more. Frankly, neither was he. She was incredible. He should have told her. From the wiped-out look in her eyes, he figured she knew.

He returned to her topic as near as he could remember it. "I've watched you before, on film. Instant replays of the horse stunt. Dancing with me on the cliff. Now I've got another vision, the look on your face when you danced beneath me."

He traced the contour of her blush, letting the light make love to her. It filtered across her, blanketing her in white, the breeze stealing its share of caresses. He had to touch where it touched, to possess what she freely gave to the night. He could do things no fantasy lover dared, making a dream he hadn't even known he had come true. He loved someone again.

The reality rushed through him, swelling his heart. He floated on air, anchored to the earth by one woman. He waited for the inevitable pain; he'd known it too long to feel comfortable without it. But it was gone. The emptiness had been filled. Lord knew he probably didn't deserve two loves in one lifetime. He'd never take this one for granted.

But with love came a host of other emotions. Protectiveness, tenderness, concern—all there in one form or another long before. All of them multiplied now. He had to keep her safe, close, warm. Nothing could mess up his second chance.

He wanted to seal it, consummate it. His arousal built slowly. He courted hers with his fingertips. He watched her lids flutter, their rhythm mimicking the flutter of the torn curtain above them. He traced the bruises he'd made when he'd gripped her to him. His kiss begged forgiveness. Her sigh told him none was necessary.

"I love you, Annie."

"I know."

"That sure, huh?"

She smiled, drowsy and satisfied. Her lips pursed, a

kiss for the night. Her hips nestled into the bed. Greg watched and waited. His lady love wasn't nearly as sleepy as she pretended. His touch had her a tad unsettled.

Annie felt a delicately delivered love bite land on her breast, the talons of a dove making off with her heart. She held her breath when he did it again, anticipation making the sensation all the more exquisite.

"I don't know if we can top that," he murmured.

"Never dare me."

He chuckled, low and dirty. He could be downright devilish. He'd been everything she'd expected and more, capable of bruising and biting and being too heavy and not apologizing. In other words, a man. The man she loved. She'd known from the start he needed her. She'd never guessed how all-consuming that need could be.

"Was I too rough?" he asked. "I can be gentle. This time."

Annie caught her breath and listened to her body. Crests of their last encounter met ripples of new desire. "You'll get carried away and we'll end up doing what we did before," she complained lightly.

A wolfish grin crinkled his features. "What a shame that would be."

Discomfort nagged her, new need. She rolled her body to meet his, unable to hide her admiration. "How do you do that? Make me want you all over again?"

They tussled a moment until he had her where he wanted her, on top. "Just good, I guess."

"Oh, no," she argued, her lips pouting, sexy and full. "You're bad, Mr. Ford. Very very bad."

❧━━━━━❧

"Was that you or a coyote howling?" she asked afterward.

Greg barked a laugh and swatted her on the behind. His fingers tracked the pale expanse of her thigh. The windmill creaked. So did the bed.

They talked in whispers, with touches. He told her the things he'd told her when she'd been asleep and couldn't hear, when he'd been inside her and she might have misunderstood a few hushed words for the heat of passion and not for what they were, the plain unvarnished truth. "I love you."

"You don't have to say that."

"I mean it, Annie." He turned her face back to him. He didn't mind her tossing her head on the pillow in the midst of lovemaking, the wilder the better. Her turning away now bothered him on a completely different level. It scared him. "Look at me. I love you. I don't know how or when, but it's been there awhile. I didn't know how to deal with it."

"You think I do?"

Her vulnerability speared him. No one would ever know her fears the way he did. From this night forward, he'd see to it she had no reason to doubt his love.

She glanced away, giving him a way out. "I take more risks than you do."

"You haven't been burned the way I have."

"That's why we'd be good together. I can barge in where angels fear to tread. Or ghosts." She touched the scar beside his eye. "You were afraid to love again; it's understandable."

"No. I was afraid of losing what I loved. I'm learning the difference. I don't ever want to lose you."

She snuggled her hip in next to his with a bump and grind, taking a chance on a smile. "I'm not going anywhere. When I've committed myself to something, I stick with it."

"Don't look back."

"Or second-guess."

"Problem is, you never know what might happen."

She kissed him quick. "There is no down side to love. Got that? It's worth every minute, and the Fates be damned."

"Live it all." He laughed, holding her to him. "Easy for you to say."

"Greg? Don't leave me."

"I'm right here."

"No, you weren't, you were miles away. What happened with Pam won't happen with us."

"I know. We'll be ninety and crotchety, and I'll be chasing you around the old folks home in a souped-up electric wheelchair."

"Or I'll be chasing you."

"Again?"

She laughed low in her throat. "Again."

Just before dawn Annie slept. Greg lay in the dark, the night's emotional roller coaster rumbling to a halt.

The doubts she'd warned him against snuck up on him. Like a classic swordfight scene, he faced down one after the other, slashing, backing up, parrying. He thought of the quicksand his stomach became whenever Annie did something dangerous. He recalled the explosion on the set, the black twisted frame of the Corvette. It looked the way his nerves felt when, for a split second, he hadn't known where she was. He remembered Dickens's jump, Annie's roll. Julie McLean's fall and her scream of pain.

He held Annie closer, pulling her across his body, nestling her head to his shoulder. He reached past her to fluff a pillow she wouldn't need, not if he kept her where he wanted her.

Just in case. It had become his life's motto, what every stunt coordinator lived by.

But stunts hadn't taken Pam from him. Life had. How could he hope to outsmart that? Annie would say outlive it, enjoy it while they could. He'd fallen into a trap he'd sworn to avoid. He loved someone again. And all he could do was pray to God she wasn't snatched out from under him.

"What's wrong?" she whispered.

He eased his hold, pulling the awful blanket up over her. "Just want to make sure you don't wander away."

"I won't sleepwalk again."

"No?"

"I think I found what I was looking for."

They snuck back to the house as the sun came up. Within an hour Rusty clanged the dinner bell. They stumbled down the stairs, voraciously consuming the breakfast he'd prepared, Annie cheerfully avoiding her father's suspicious stare.

At eight Annie and Greg piled into the pickup. Rusty frowned when Annie clambered in without waiting for Greg to open the door for her. Resting his gnarled hands on the wheelchair's brakes, he momentarily refused to shake the younger man's offered hand. "Is that any way to treat a lady?"

Greg shrugged. "Don't look at me. I didn't raise her."

Annie hooted, her elbow balanced in the truck's open window. "He's got you there, Dad!"

The old man scowled. "Be gone. Both of you. And drive safe."

"Yes, Dad."

"And tell them boys at the studio they could use a lovable galoot in a wheelchair sometime."

"I will, Dad."

"And look out for the speed trap south of Barstow."

"Yes, Dad," Greg grumbled.

Annie laughed, waving good-bye until the dust kicked up by the tires obscured the ranch and they turned onto the highway.

"When we are due in L.A.?" she asked.

"Noon appointment at the studio."

"Cutting it close."

"Mm."

Annie had seen Greg grumpy before, but she'd never seen him the morning after making love. Her feminine instincts said play it cool. Unfortunately, those instincts had always taken a back seat to sheer pugnaciousness. She'd rather face a fear than hide behind it. "We'll have to talk about last night sooner or later."

"Yeah?"

Ten miles elapsed.

"Looks like later," she muttered, resting her chin on her hand as she watched the cactus roll by. "Hands up, pardner," she called to a saguaro.

The minute she noticed it, Greg's smile turned flatter than the yellow lines on the road. His silence gnawed at her resolve. He'd said he loved her. He'd promised. The words sounded hopeful and dewy-eyed when whispered in her heart. She wanted to wrestle this out, confront him, stop him from retreating into his shell. She studied the hard set of his jaw and knew she'd have as much success butting heads with a ram.

Meanwhile she had a few truths she needed to face herself. A cautious, tentative love might be all he was capable of. Could a woman who leapt wholeheartedly deal with a man who didn't? He controlled every aspect of his life and work, only to lose it in a night of soul-searing passion. Would a hundred precious nights like those be enough?

From the beginning she'd needed enough faith for both of them. A little gumption could overcome insecurity any day. She loved him and she had his word for it, he loved her. Greg Ford didn't lie.

Wriggling in her seat belt, she curled her legs under her on the vinyl seat.

"It's not as safe that way," he observed.

She pulled the shoulder belt between her breasts. "I know." Elbow balanced on the seat back, she snaked her arm across the gap, absently stroking the side of his face.

"Annie."

She hadn't heard that warning tone since the previous night, when she'd put her hand somewhere he hadn't expected. She'd taken charge for a moment, made him relax, accept, delight. She had other motives in mind now. Her fingertip drew an arc beneath the crescent scar on his temple. "How did you get this?"

"Horseshoe."

She winced. "A horse kicked you?"

His hands tightened on the wheel. "I was playing horseshoes, arguing with some guy over who was closer to the post. When I lay down to eyeball it, some yoyo tossed another one."

"Ouch."

He broke down and laughed. "Need I mention we were all drunker than skunks? My wild and crazy days on the ranch."

Annie remembered a wild and crazy night. She grazed the gash on his chin. "And this?"

"Steering wheel. Car-chase scene."

"Ooh."

Despite the lack of oncoming traffic, the road demanded his complete attention. Or so he wanted her to believe. Annie glanced at the side-view mirror. They had the highway to themselves as far as the eye could see.

"And this?" Her fingers rested on the pulse on the far side of his neck.

"That's not a scar."

"What is it?"

He swallowed. "A love bite from last night."

She pressed lightly. His pulse pounded back.

"Annie. I've gotta drive."

"I'm curious."

He briskly described the others before her probing hands went searching. "The one you were looking for beneath my ear is from a broken bottle in a saloon scene, the one on my shoulder from a retractable knife that didn't, and the one on my shin from a bad break in a motorcycle stunt. The bone punctured the skin."

That unwholesome detail didn't faze Annie in the least. She slid her hand to his chest and rested it over his heart. "And this one?" she asked quietly.

The deepest scar of all. He looked at her as long as he dared. On this road a man could see for miles. And sometimes he couldn't see what was right before him. "They don't go away, Silk."

"Ever?"

"They fade."

The way love sometimes did? Annie guessed at what he didn't say. In the light of day, scars showed clearer, the risks loomed larger. He had a past; she had to take that into account. Overcoming it, accepting him faults and all, could make their own love richer, closer, deeper. And infinitely more precarious.

"No one ever said it would be easy," she said.

"It isn't." He looked at her until the road called him back. Reaching over, he sought her hand, settling it on his thigh. "But it's worth it."

She smiled, that cocky dare-anything grin. "I believe that. Risks add spice to life."

An idea narrowed his eyes to a crafty squint. "Want to spice it up right now?"

"How?"

The lady loved a dare. Greg took full advantage, slowly rubbing the back of her hand up and down his thigh. He unbuckled her belt and slid her over on the seat next to him.

"Is it safe to drive like this?" she asked minutes later.

"Trust me. I'm a professional."

Maybe Greg Ford didn't lie, Annie thought, but she'd never heard him stretch the truth the way he did at the studio. Breaking the bad news to the executive they'd borrowed the Corvette from, Greg played with facts as if they were Silly Putty. For all the executive knew, an asteroid might have pulverized his car, or a herd of stampeding bison crushed it.

Annie backed up Greg's version one hundred percent. Batting her lashes, she looked contrite, earnest, diligent, and enthusiastic by turns.

The executive squirmed in his chair. "I've been using a studio loaner for three weeks now. You want to take that away too?"

"All we need," Greg promised, "is a matching Corvette, silver, early '90s model. Six days at the most."

"Uh, I don't know."

"Exterior shots only. No explosives anywhere near it."

The man's sandy brows rose to within inches of his slicked-back hair. "I thought you said a herd of bison—"

Annie jumped up, settling her neat little seat on the edge of the man's desk. In minutes, she'd buttered him up thicker than a Thanksgiving turkey. "It's for this one itty-bitty scene. I'll never let it out of my sight." Where she'd learned that kittenish tone, heaven only knew.

Greg practically choked.

The executive relented. "No stunts."

"Exterior shots only," Annie promised.

Minutes later she pranced down the hall and into the elevator, dangling a set of car keys under Greg's nose. "Honey works better than vinegar."

"Let's get out of here before he hears what really happened."

They raced to the studio parking lot, handing the keys to a valet. "One Corvette to go, please."

"Yes, ma'am!"

————————◆————————◆

"You've driven one before?" Greg asked doubt-fully as Annie hopped into the Corvette the next morn-ing. He'd take the truck because he didn't trust it. It could be temperamental. But the Corvette was new, less familiar for her.

Annie had heard this rationale twice already. "Ford, I know how to drive."

He planted both elbows on the door, leaning in to give her a kiss. "You certainly drive me crazy."

The love they'd made had been exhausting, exhila-rating, exquisite. She sighed at the memory. "Have I told you how *extremely* happy you make me?"

"Oh, a few hundred times."

She gave him a quick peck on the lips and revved the engine, throwing the stick shift into reverse. "Last one to Arizona's a rotten egg."

"Hey!"

She braked with a squeal of rubber. "You know the way back? You need a map? Shall we synchronize our watches?"

A scowl fought a losing battle with his smile. "You take the high desert, I'll take the low desert."

"And I'll be in Arizona before you. Bye." She blew him a kiss and took off down the street.

Slowing for a red light, she happily nosed through the box of CDs the executive had left behind. She familiarized herself with the car, noting some play in the brakes and a tendency to pull to the right. Her high-performance-driving classes had taught her how to handle almost anything. Not that Greg would believe it. Not that she worried too much about convincing him either. He had professionalism in spades; the man needed to pick up on some of her playfulness first.

He'd certainly been playful the night before. Annie's throat went dry at the very idea. She swung into a drive-through restaurant, winked at a couple of teenage boys for ogling the car more than her, and picked up a coffee for the trip east. She'd be in Arizona by nine P.M. Too bad she and Greg had to take the fourteen-hour trip separately. They'd gotten very little talking done on the drive to L.A. But their lovemaking had spoken volumes.

On her father's ranch they'd burned. At Greg's apartment they'd taken their time, savoring each other and their newfound love. He could be a gentle and thorough lover, as painstaking about her pleasure as her safety. He'd never asked about birth control, taking precautions as a matter of course. He'd also demanded more than any man she'd known. Absolute honesty, total concentration, stunning responsiveness.

"And consideration," she said aloud, sipping her coffee.

Her tour of his apartment had been a perfect example of consideration. She'd grinned at his self-consciousness when he'd opened the door.

"It's nothing special. Probably a mess. I don't remember what state it was in when I left for the location."

His place was fine if nondescript. Off-white walls, a window overlooking the Hollywood hills, a few framed posters of films he'd worked on, most of them featuring action scenes, careening cars, or brawling cowboys. While he flipped through his unopened mail, she wandered off to explore.

The bedroom drew her. Sun streamed into the hallway from its large windows. A brightly patched quilt covered the king-size bed. Pictures of a laughing brunette framed the bureau mirror.

Standing in the doorway, Greg cleared his throat. "I forgot about those."

Annie shrugged, crossed her arms. "They've been here a long time." Longer than I have, she'd thought.

"They're only pictures. What's in here is what matters." He lay a hand over his chest. Then he took Annie in his arms. "I loved her. But I love you too. Always will. If you'll let me."

She'd wrapped her arms around him, clasping him tight. "I love you."

"I don't want to lose you."

"You won't."

One hundred miles east of L.A., Annie changed the CD, glancing in her rearview mirror as she did so. "Lose you? I can't even shake you for two hours!"

The boss hadn't meant a word of it when he'd said she could take her own route to Arizona. His truck was two hundred yards behind her and closing.

She slowed down. He slowed down.

She sped up. He kept up.

The overprotective so-and-so wasn't letting her out of his sight.

Annie fumed. Then laughed. "Am I going to have you hovering over me for the rest of my life?" She'd never thought she'd like that, but for the life of her she couldn't shake the sweet feeling that came with it. He loved her, he really did.

She downshifted and sped around a tractor trailer. "You're going to have some fun keeping up with me, Ford."

Seventy-five was barely speeding on high, dry roads, ruler-straight and blessedly unclogged with L.A. traffic. Or so Annie rationalized. Let fussy Mr. Ford follow her trail; she'd beat him to Monument Valley with time to spare. And tonight, in his hotel room or hers, she'd teach him a thing or two about holding on tight.

"You're never going to lose me, Ford. Never."

TWELVE

"Silk," Greg muttered, staring at the steam spewing out of his radiator cap.

"Just a rag, really," the gas station attendant said, handing him a red piece of cloth. "We'll get some water in there and she'll be good as new."

Greg wiped the back of his neck with the cloth, inhaling its gas fumes. This was no time for his rickety old truck to give out on him. That he'd given Annie the Corvette for this reason was little consolation.

He popped the top on a grape soda and grit his teeth against the sugary taste. His lady love would laugh her ivory blond head off over this one. He could see her sassy sway as he entered the cantina, an hour behind her at least. She'd sashay up and present him with a loser's kiss.

Out there in the blinding sun, the idea actually appealed to him. Losing didn't matter. Loving her did.

He caught up with her at sunset. Coming out of the San Francisco mountains north of Flagstaff, he sighted the silver Corvette he'd chased all day. A tank-sized old Cadillac was playing tag with her, its teenage occupants waving out the window as they passed, braked, ducked back in behind her, and generally drove like jerks. Greg watched, pushing his four-wheel pile of useless metal harder to close the distance.

Going up a steep grade, the teenagers chose the moment to pull out and pass for good. As they came even with her, a semi loomed over the crest, bearing down in the oncoming lane.

Half a mile back, Greg gripped his steering wheel so tight, the leather squeaked. The sixteen-wheeler slammed on its brakes and went into a sidewinder skid, blocking both lanes. The Caddy fishtailed. The Corvette's brakes flashed. Annie swerved hard right, purposely letting the Caddy squeak between her and the truck as her own car careened off the road. She hit the shoulder going seventy-five.

Helpless, all Greg saw was a plume of dust. All he heard were the hoarse cries of a man screaming "No!" and the dull thud of a fist pounding the wheel.

Annie wrestled the Corvette back onto the shoulder as if she drove like a banshee every day of the week. Coasting to a halt on the edge of the road, she waited five seconds for the dust to settle, then unhooked her belt and got out. The adrenaline had yet to kick in.

While Greg's truck rolled to a stop ten yards behind her, she took a minute to walk around the car. The paint job looked fine, considering.

"Did that qualify as a stunt?" she asked out loud. Shaking her head, she perched her rear end against the driver's-side door and flashed Greg a smile as he walked cautiously toward her. "A few dings from some stones, but I don't think we hurt it too much. Bet you thought we'd lost another Corvette."

His expression was unreadable. He inspected the car himself. "Looks fine. Kids?"

"Kids. The Caddy's long gone. Thankfully, no-body got hurt. Could've been worse." Who'd know that better than Greg? Annie rushed to explain. "It was a swerve, a controlled skid. No problem."

"I know. I saw. Why don't you follow me back to the hotel? We should be there in an hour and a half."

It took two with Greg driving fifty-five all the way. Annie wasn't complaining. She had more than enough time to remember the gauntness of his features, the gray tinge beneath his skin. The near miss had scared him more than her. The minute they got back to the hotel, she'd reassure him. "It was fine," she rehearsed, "I'm fine. Nothing bad's going to happen to me. I can handle it."

He didn't give her a chance to say any of it. When they reached his room he unlocked it, swinging the door open for both of them to enter.

"Inviting me in?" she joked, her heart pumping.

"I want you to stay."

Her adrenaline found a new reason to flow. She slipped inside. "Greg, I know what almost happened today. I know it scared you. But it's okay. It worked out. I'm not Pam and I'm not going to die in some accident. I know you're worried about losing me suddenly. But didn't you see? I'm a professional. Trust me."

He closed in on her as she spoke. "I know all of that, Annie. I don't want to talk about it." The lines around his mouth revealed his strain. So did his hoarse request. "Take off your blouse. Please."

She stopped on a hiccup of surprise. "All right." Her fingers trembled as she undid the buttons one at a time. He looked at her as if her couldn't get enough of her. He hadn't heard a word she'd said.

Closing the blinds, he turned on the bathroom light, leaving the door open an inch. He nodded to the switch behind her and she flicked it off. As her eyes grew accustomed to the only remaining swath of light, he emerged from the shadows.

"I've seen you on the screen, on the set, in my bed. I want to watch you tonight."

She nodded, lowering the blouse around her shoulders. She couldn't tease, couldn't do this for play. It meant too much to him. Convincing him everything was fine meant everything to her.

But the words wouldn't come. She fussed with the button on her jeans. A fingernail chattered against the zipper as it opened. Her skin tingled with cold in a stuffy room closed up for two days. And two hot nights.

They'd spent those nights in other beds, in each other's arms. Tonight was different. He needed her more than ever. But he kept his distance.

"How much more?" she asked.

"I'll tell you when to stop."

She walked over to a straight-backed chair and sat, pulling off her short boots and socks. Her legs quaked when she slipped down her jeans. The previously dark room seemed alive with motes of light, zinging against her bared skin.

She stepped forward, her hand glancing lightly over the brass bedframe, the cold metal almost sizzling beneath her hot fingers. She squared her shoulders, feeling the skim of a silk chemise against her nipples. She reached for the hem, ready to lift it over her head.

He reached out of the darkness and touched her waist. She inhaled sharply. "Go on," he said.

She lifted it higher, feeling naked before him, feeling unaccountably alone.

He cupped her breast. "Go on."

She drew it past her hair and let the soft fabric fall to the floor. Greg's hands drew her panties down. They hushed silently around her ankles. When she stepped out of them, he turned her.

Her eyes fluttered shut as he skimmed his fingers down her back, touching places she'd never thought of as erotic, the underside of her shoulder blades, the expanse of skin beside her navel. There were other places he knew only too well. He touched those next.

She couldn't stand it anymore, couldn't stand by while he treated her as if she were some perfect statue. "Greg."

"Sh."

"Don't shush me," she whispered urgently, putting her arms around his neck. "It's all right. Something terrible almost happened today. *Almost*. But it didn't.

"I love you."

Her heart cracked. How could that sound so final? "I'm fine. Nothing's going to go wrong."

"You don't know that."

"I believe it. We're pros at this, we can handle anything. Heck, we make accidents happen."

He mangled a fistful of her hair before letting it slip through his fingers. "Not always."

"What happened to Pam—"

"Doesn't have anything to do with us. Not tonight. Kiss me, Annie. Give me tonight."

She clasped her arms around him, giving him a drowning, breath-stealing, life-challenging kiss he'd never forget. "I love you. Every night."

His hands raced over her, molding her to him, every now and then holding her away to feast on her with his eyes. "Will you do anything I ask?"

His hunger made her tremble. Her heart tripped. "Anything."

He laughed dryly, tipping up her chin with his thumb. "My Annie, nervous."

It wasn't his lovemaking she feared. Something was wrong, something in the way he touched her, worshiped her as if from afar. She clutched his hand to her breast and let the swell of her heartbeat pound home. She was there, alive, loving.

And he wouldn't talk to her.

He laid her down on the bed and stood beside it, skimming her body with his gaze, roughly stripping off his shirt. Her doubts crumbled. They'd talk in the morning. They had a lifetime to talk.

She made sure he knew it in a dozen different ways, until dawn tinged her skin with hazy pink, and their bodies glistened with sweat.

Annie awoke with a start. Fully dressed, Greg sat at the foot of the bed, one of her feet resting on his lap. He'd stretched one leg alongside her body.

"Didn't your mother teach you any manners?" she griped, shoving his cowboy boot off the bed.

He lazily returned it. "If she'd seen me with you last night, she'd disown me."

Annie scowled darkly. "Mothers know nothing about the kinds of things we did last night."

His chuckle rasped like a rusty lock.

Her smile faded. In the dark she'd been able to pretend she didn't see that worried look, the good-bye look. "What time is it?"

"Five A.M."

They had an hour before reporting to the set. That gave her plenty of time to say what she had to say. "Greg, what happened yesterday—"

He stroked the arch in her foot as if he were a sculptor in love with the shape of a stone.

"Stop playing with my toes and listen. Yesterday was an accident."

"A nearly fatal one."

"But it wasn't."

"It could have been."

"It wasn't." Clenching the sheet, she sat up, heedless of her bare breasts, the badly twisted cotton draped across her lap. "Things like that don't happen every day."

"They do if you're a stuntwoman."

"I *knew* you'd bring that up sooner or later. You know as well as I do the average American highway is more dangerous than any stunt."

"I agree. You know what you're doing on the job. You have the training, the smarts, the balls. If you don't mind my saying so."

"I consider it a high compliment."

He quirked his mouth into the semblance of a smile. Annie *had* to get through to him. He was entirely too calm about this. As if nothing and no one could change his mind. "Greg, I won't get killed."

"Don't make promises you can't keep." He sounded so tired, so sure.

Annie felt all the air leave the room. This place had been filled with love and giving only the night before. She'd given him everything, knowing deep in her soul that he'd do exactly this—give it all right back and send her on her way.

How could it hurt so badly when she'd seen it coming? How did he manage to make her so furious while remaining so all-fired calm?

Striking out when angry wasn't one of her best traits, but Annie was a fighter. She wouldn't quit now. "So you're running away."

A pained smile crossed his face. He refused to take the bait. "I can't do it, Annie. I can't love someone and have them ripped away from me. I can't risk it."

He caressed her ankle as if it were priceless marble. She leaned forward, molding his hand around it until the pulse beat undeniably strong. "Too late," she declared. "You love me and you'll have to take what comes, the same as the rest of us."

His jaw clenched, the flash of anger as fleeting as a shadow. "It hurts like hell letting you go, believe me. But it doesn't hurt half as much as losing you forever. If you walk away, at least I'll know you're out there somewhere."

She jerked her foot out of his grip with an unlady-like curse and threw off the sheet. Storming around the bedroom, she found pieces of clothing everywhere. None of them did her any good without underwear. She got dressed anyway, punching her arm into a shirtsleeve without a chemise, kicking into her jeans without her panties. He'd have to find them later. She hoped he felt good and sorry for himself when he did.

"You got it," she spat. "Run and hide in your

self-protective hole. Don't risk being alive, don't risk loving somebody because it might not work out exactly the way you planned it in the shooting script."

"Annie."

"Don't say it. You love me. That's a damn sorry excuse for leaving me."

"I know."

"So what are you going to do about it?" She stood there half-zipped, half-buttoned, her hair a nest of tangles, her lips puffy and pink. Tears of sheer frustration broke free. "Well?"

Greg couldn't take his eyes off her. "I'm going to walk you through your last stunt, then say good-bye."

"Is that it?"

Her strangled voice cut into him. His own was smooth and cold as stone. "Don't fight me on this, Annie, you can't win."

Stomping her feet into her boots, she spied a scrap of silk wound around her heel. Crumpling it in one hand, she strode to the door. "So this is how long your 'always' lasts."

"Death lasts longer."

Her shoulders slumped. She leaned her forehead against the door. "Don't you get it? That's what makes love so precious."

He didn't reply. She closed the door behind her and opened her own on the other side of the hall. She didn't report to the set for two days.

———————

Annie stood beside the folding table outside the trailer, listening while Greg explained the final day of shooting. He looked awful. Bruise-dark circles ringed his eyes, his cheeks were creased. The tension she'd wanted to ease in him since her first day on the job had become twice as taut, the man himself twice as unhappy and lonely.

Because he couldn't face losing two women, she thought. She'd spent forty-eight hours trying to understand that. It made no sense for him to love a stuntwoman when he'd already lost a wife. Annie couldn't really hold that against him. Could she?

"We're going to burn down the stable," he said. Clenching a pencil, he traced rapidly over the diagram, explaining every point. "They trailered all but two horses back to Hollywood yesterday. The remaining pair will have handlers standing by, ready to blindfold them and lead them out as the fake smoke is piped in. After that, the focus shifts to the woman trapped in the hayloft during the fire."

"That's me," she quipped. "A fiery woman."

The men chuckled.

Greg continued, his concentration unshakable. He rubbed the scar on his chin and got back to business. "The fire will be set in these corners. As Chris and Jackson duke it out, the ladder to the loft is kicked away. Listen up, Jackson."

"I got it."

"Chris, you get impaled by the pitchfork and fall back into this stall. Crawl out through the opening we cut here."

"Thanks for not burning me alive, boss."

"You're welcome. We've set up fans to send the smoke billowing to the left so the cameras get a clear shot of the stable floor and ladder. A crane will raise another camera to the upper window so we can cover the action in the hayloft."

"A lot of action in haylofts," Bill quipped.

"Pay attention. Beams fall here and here. Walls are rigged to collapse here and here." Greg paused. "Absolute concentration is required."

Belinda Saint had spent two days screaming for help while fake smoke rose through the slats. It was Annie's turn to actually escape the burning building. She stared at Greg instead of the diagram. "Got it," she said, because he was looking at her, because her safety was vital to him. But not her love.

"Fire's pretty unpredictable," he warned.

"Yes, it is." Her husky voice was suggestive and sorrowful at once.

"It's important that you understand."

"I'm trying."

Every man at the table watched them, two miserable people trying to do their jobs. Jackson squirmed inside his leather jacket, drumming his fingers against a motorcycle helmet tucked beneath his arm. He squinted at Amos. The hefty black man shrugged and glanced at Chris. Chris scratched his brush cut and looked at Bill. Bill grimaced at Tony. Tony pursed his lips, whistling a mournful Spanish tune.

Annie wanted to scream at them to do something, to talk some sense into their stubborn, mule-headed boss. They just shuffled their feet and awaited further instructions.

Greg explained where the rest of the crew would be stationed, manning fire extinguishers and hoses. He cleared the gravel out of his throat before turning to Annie again. "We've got new wood here. The stain applied to make it look weathered might catch quick. Once that burns off, the wood itself may smolder, making it hard for you to see."

Annie saw only him. "I can handle it."

"I want to be sure you're okay with this."

The way her heart hurt, she wasn't so sure. "You can't always predict what will happen."

"That's why we're talking about it now."

"Are we?"

Greg stood his ground, staring at her as if it hurt to look at her. It did.

Jackson quickly disengaged himself from the group, cutting off the production assistant before he could get within nagging range. "You ready to go, Ford?" the little man yelled.

Greg stared at Annie, protecting her from feeling rushed, standing between her and anything that might hurry her. "We've got all morning to walk through this, you know."

"Then what?"

They both knew what—it'd be over. The filming, the relationship, the affair. Was that all it had been?

"Keep talking," Annie said, turning once more to the diagram.

He tapped a pencil against the table for a count of ten, then tore his gaze away from her. He strafed the rest of the crew with a laserlike glare, coming to a halt on Amos. "She'll be depending on you and Tony. You two run in, put the ladder back, and climb up to her. Amos, you get to the top and take a bullet in the back. Try not to knock Tony off the rungs below when you fall to the floor."

"Wouldn't dream of it," Amos said.

"Tony, you get the rest of the way up, take her in your arms, and bring her down."

"With pleasure." Tony's Latin-lover leer went over like a lead balloon.

Annie barely managed a grin. Her cheeks were too puffy to rise, her eyes too red to twinkle. "I take it I'm screaming and struggling the whole time?"

"You're holding on for dear life."

"Yes, I am."

Greg's jaw clenched. He began to say something, but thought better of it. Wrapping up with a few terse commands, he sent the crew to the stables at the other end of town. Annie hung behind.

"You told me once to come to you if I was scared," she said. "I am."

"You can do this."

His vote of confidence hurt more than it helped.

Why couldn't he have confidence in *them*? "What scares me most is losing you and not being able to do anything about it."

"Annie."

"I can handle anything that comes my way. Didn't I prove that yesterday at seventy miles an hour?"

"Seventy-five. All you proved was that fate can't be trusted. I can't risk it, Annie." He tucked the shooting script under one arm and stuffed his stopwatch in his shirt pocket next to a crumpled cigarette pack.

Her heart sank, but anger rose to meet it. "I don't suppose it'd be much of a marriage anyway."

Settling his Stetson on his head, he eyed her warily from under the brim. "What do you mean?"

"You'd probably keep me barefoot and pregnant all the time, so you'd know I was safe cooped up in a house somewhere."

"It's a thought."

She huffed at his grim smile and hugged herself tight. They strolled toward the stables together. "You'd probably never let me leave the house at night."

"Not alone."

"There'd be a shotgun beside the bed in case of burglars."

"No guns in the house."

"Right. Not safe. Of course, there'd be a state-of-the-art alarm system."

"I'd design it myself."

"And you'd drive me everywhere. Put safety mats

in the bathtubs. Circuit breakers on every electric outlet."

He almost laughed at her fantasy. The truth cut deeper.

"You can't keep me safe, no matter how many precautions you take," she said.

"My point exactly."

"Mine too." She stopped in the middle of the street, the toe of her boot scuffing the dirt. "Greg, I have an announcement to make. I'm going to die."

He rudely stepped on her next line. "Everybody does."

So much for shock tactics. She stalked after him, fighting the urge to wave her arms, rant and rave. "But I don't let it stop me from living. You do!"

He paused at the camera line. He actually had the nerve to turn and kiss her on the cheek.

His lips found empty air. "Never mind," she hissed. "I can't talk to you."

Head down, fists clenched, she marched into the stable, ignoring the solicitous looks of the stuntmen taking their places. The fragrant dimness enveloped her. "You think I'm giving up?" she muttered to the trampled ground. He'd thrown her harder than any horse when he'd told her this was over. His quiet determination to have her out of his life had knocked the wind out of her and very nearly the fight as well.

Not for long. She'd gone over the accident a hundred times, reliving their last night together and every night before that. She'd thought back over every conversation they'd had, every touch shared, every desperate kiss.

Like a bird flapping its way through a storm, she'd come to rest at last on one of the last things he'd said as she'd stood at the door to his room ready to leave him. *"Don't fight me on this, Annie, you can't win."*

He knew she couldn't resist a challenge. Yet he'd handed her one. The question was, how to meet it before the movie was finished?

THIRTEEN

"You guys are useless."

"Yeah, but it doesn't matter 'cause you don't love us." Amos studied his unhappy colleague as she sat in a pile of straw in the hayloft.

"You've known him longer than I have."

"Not that way," Tony chirped.

Annie dangled her feet over the edge, squinting as cameramen angled a huge light reflector into place, directing more light into the stable.

Like a couple of overgrown boys, Amos and Tony ran up and down the ladder, yanking at each other's heels, throwing themselves off, tucking and rolling as they hit the ground. Annie and Cody had played the same way. She wished she could join them.

But when Amos grabbed his back as if shot and executed a lovely dead man's leap into a hay pile, all Annie remembered were Greg's fingers skimming her spine. Maybe a dying-swan scene would convince him how much he really loved her.

Not a chance. It would only remind him how much he had to lose.

"But he'll lose me if he doesn't wise up!"

Amos and Tony couldn't help.

She concentrated on what came next. Unfortunately, playing "the girl" in this scene meant all she had to do was resist being saved. Kind of the way Greg Ford resisted being loved. The man was maddening.

A megaphone barked out a staticky mush of unintelligible orders. The production assistant scuttled around the side of the stable, walkie-talkie in hand. He peered into the barn for Greg. One of the remaining horses nuzzled the side of his head. He yelped and jumped aside. "When do we get this show on the road?"

"Almost finished," Greg yelled, riding a camera crane up to the hayloft from the outside.

The production assistant scampered after him.

Annie whirled as Greg tapped on the window. She opened it. He directed the boom closer, judging angles. "Annie, move to your left. Okay, hold on."

Her heart dipped when she realized what he intended to do. They were twenty feet up with no safety net. With no more regard than a man jumping over a crack in a sidewalk, he crouched, then leapt.

Annie brushed straw off the seat of her corduroy skirt. A high-collared blouse with a cameo brooch completed her outfit from Costuming. "Pretty daring move, Ford. Did you practice it?"

"You're looking ladylike today."

"Just try me."

Wrapped up in his work, he reeled off a list of details, referring to a page paperclipped to his script. Half the orders were shouted outside to the cameraman, the other half to her. "Stay within this radius, or you'll be out of the shot."

"Fine."

"Amos, we need to see your face over the rim here, yeah, chest-high, that'll get it. Tony, the other camera will catch you until you pass this point. Then you rescue Annie and carry her down." He ran through it twice more. Finally he asked for questions.

"That should do it, boss," Tony said.

"We can do it," Annie added.

"Great. I want to walk through it one more time."

Annie and Tony traded looks. "Greg, we've got it."

He looked up at her as he backed down the ladder. "We walk through it until I'm satisfied."

She threw up her hands. "Walk, run, skip, jump. I'll sit here and resist."

Tony followed Greg down, omitting the last few rungs as he hopped to the stable floor. A grunt of pain froze everyone in place. Annie scampered to the edge of the loft and peered over, her blood chilled, her heart hammering. "What happened?"

Grimacing, Tony hopped toward a post, muttering a series of Spanish curses.

"He twisted his ankle," Greg shouted.

Tony repaid him with a Spanish expletive.

"Tony," Annie cooed from her perch, "it's the women who're supposed to turn their ankles in these scenes, not their rescuers."

Tony let go of the post long enough to send her an unflattering gesture. She chuckled. Greg glared.

"Now what, boss?"

He scowled up at her. "We'll have to run through it with me in his place."

Annie rolled her eyes. "You explained it to Tony three times. Can't we just do it?"

"Humor me."

"When it comes to stunts, you have no sense of humor whatsoever. That's a known fact, Ford."

"Tough."

Reclining in the straw, Annie listened to the fight scene carrying on below. "Stupid man," she muttered to herself.

The loft shook when Amos hurled himself off the ladder.

"Stupid, stubborn, aggravating man!" And so silly of her to want to wail over something she couldn't control. If he didn't love her, fine, she was woman enough to walk away.

But he loves you and you know it.

"Ready?"

She caught her breath, instantly irritated at his

impatient frown as he cleared the top of the ladder. He didn't look any happier than she did. "What exactly did you have in mind?"

"I want you to pay attention."

She skimmed the scar on his cheek with her fingertips. Her voice turned breathy, her eyes full of pain. "I am."

His eyes darkened. But there was no time to spare. He picked her up with a grunt and backed toward the ladder.

She wound her arms loosely around his unyielding, unreasonable, thoroughly stiff neck. "Wouldn't want to fall for me, huh?" She hated teasing anyone in so much internal pain, but making him smile had been her goal since she'd got there. She wouldn't quit now.

All the way down he kept her safely compressed between him and the ladder. On the stable floor he whirled her in his arms and raced for the door, ducking a beam rigged to crash down as they passed. The bored camera crew sent up a desultory cheer as they emerged into the daylight.

"Okay," Greg muttered, setting her on her feet. "Do it again."

"Again?"

"Again."

She climbed back up the ladder. Stretched in the hay, she yawned as Greg and Amos ran through the shoot-out. Once more Greg appeared at the edge of the loft. "My hero," she said with a sigh.

They backed down the ladder. They raced outside.

In the baking sunlight, the production assistant paced. "Now?" he whined.

"One more time," Greg said.

Annie grimly climbed the ladder, grumbling at Greg all the way. "What's supposed to save me from you and your blessed rehearsals?"

"Absolutely nothing."

"Ha." She lay back with all the allure of a sack of flour.

Greg got down on one knee beside her. While the crane hovered outside the window, he gently picked straw from her hair. "You could poke your eye out with this, you know."

Her heart stilled at his tone. "Would you care?"

"More than any reasonable man should."

"Whoever said you were reasonable? You're painstaking, meticulous, supremely irritating—"

"I try."

She couldn't keep up this pretense any longer, not when he stroked her hair that way. "And you love me. Admit it."

He brushed a kiss across her lips. "I try."

She broke away with a sob. "Then why are you giving up on us? What good is loving someone if you won't stand by them? Dammit, you're making me cry again."

He handed her a handkerchief, letting her be while she swiped at tears that wouldn't stop.

He'd figured it out about the same time he realized he'd have to carry her down the ladder again. He had to make sure she was all right. There simply wasn't any alternative. He couldn't walk away while she took risks alone, physical *or* emotional. He had to be there to walk her through it, always. If death darkened the edges of their future, it wouldn't dim the love.

So what if he went over budget and over schedule? So what if he exceeded every boundary he'd placed around his heart? If it meant spending a lifetime worrying about her, so be it.

"How much time is this going to take?" The production assistant protested from the foot of the ladder.

"All the time in the world," Greg replied.

Annie barely heard him, vigorously blowing her nose.

He pulled out the stopwatch Pam had given him, scraping his thumb across the inscription. *Time enough*, it read. There hadn't been enough time for him and Pam. There was for him and Annie—if he had the guts to seize it.

Light glinted off the scratched watch face, casting a dazzling beam on Annie's glimmering hair, the tears shining on her face. Greg squinted at the window. "You sure know how to give a man a sign."

"What?" Annie blew her nose again.

Greg tugged the edge of the hankie. "If Amos and I mistime our fight, if the smoke gets too thick up here or the fire too hot, wave this and we'll douse everything immediately. Got that?"

A flag of surrender. She waved it for him.

For a second he almost reached for her. Instead he sat back on his heel. "One more time."

"But they're screaming for your scalp."

"I want to be sure you're okay."

"I'm fine."

"Your eyes are red, your nose is running, and you can't keep your mind on the damn script for two seconds."

"I love you, okay? I'm miserable."

"That's all I wanted to hear." He hauled her into his arms. "I pick you up."

"Right, boss," she grumbled.

"We back to the ladder."

"Got it."

His grip tightened; he held her in close. "I'm not letting you do this alone. Understand? I'd never let you do it alone."

Her arms around his neck as he stepped down another rung, she lifted her face to him. A curious smile matched the light dawning in her eyes.

His caring, his caution, his attention to detail and to her, all added up to something he should have seen ages ago. "I'm here for you," he said gruffly, fighting an aggravating lump in his throat. "Got that?"

"Yes, boss." She practically beamed.

"When we do this for real, you hold on to me. You don't wriggle, you don't help. Not one twist extra, not one risk more."

She nodded so hard, two fat tears rolled down her cheeks. "Yes, boss."

How could he resist her? How could he have ever thought of looking life in the eye and saying, "No thanks, had enough?"

At the bottom of the ladder he tucked her head against his shoulder and raced for the door. In the brilliant sunlight he twirled her once, twice, three times, until they were both dizzy and laughing like fools. He let out a whoop. She threw his hat in the air.

The crew gaped. Annie didn't care. She swayed as he set her on her feet. He caught her; he'd always catch her.

"When the dust settles and the stunts are done, you're coming back to my room."

"Yes, boss."

"And you're going to marry me."

"In your room? I mean, yes, boss."

"Do you have anything else to say?"

Annie tilted her head, the sassy glint glowing in her eye as her mouth tilted in a knowing smile. "For a broken-down old cowboy, you sure know how to sweet-talk a lady." She rose up on tiptoe and kissed her hard-as-nails hero until they practically melted in the midday sun.

The production assistant cleared his throat. He coughed. He wheezed.

"You got asthma?" Greg asked.

"Are we ready now?"

"Almost." Greg handed Annie the stopwatch. "Lucky charm."

Time enough, she read. She touched the scar beside his eye.

He moved her hand to his heartbeat. "It always worked for me."

"Then it'll work for us. Timing is everything, you know."

"Love is." He kissed her again. "Silk?"

"Yeah?"

"Let's do it."

EPILOGUE

The helicopter beat its way across the indigo morning sky, temporarily stranding a group of people silhouetted on the sandstone pillar that towered at the edge of Monument Valley. On this needle's peak Annie and Greg would celebrate their wedding.

Rich mauves and jeweled reds slashed the horizon, promising a blazing day. The minister gingerly opened his Bible. Wind riffled the pages. He clutched the book to his chest. "Shall we proceed?" he asked in a reedy voice.

Rusty Cartwright rolled forward, giving his daughter's hand in marriage. Lowering the wheelchair from the helicopter had been the scariest part of all. Greg should have never told the old man how impossible, dangerous, and hair-raising it would be.

As Rusty joined the other guests, Greg tucked

Annie's hand in the crook of his arm. "Never tell a stuntman something's impossible," he whispered.

"Never tell his daughter that either," she retorted with a grin.

The five crewmen stood at attention in matching tuxedos and identical grins. The minister flubbed his lines every time the wind reminded him how close they stood to Heaven.

"If you want," Greg drawled, "we can call this a rehearsal and come back some other time."

The man nearly squeaked. "Repeat after me. 'With this ring—'"

Greg gripped Annie's hand. "I love you," he said, refusing for once to follow the script. He'd already insisted they take out the line "till death do us part." This one was forever.

"You may now kiss the bride," the minister said.

Annie grinned again. Greg wrapped his arms around her. They kissed. They clung.

Jackson pushed a button on a boom box, Amos popped a cork, and the party commenced. Reading the most calming passages he could find, the minister twisted his stole in one hand. Rusty chuckled, holding out his glass for a refill.

Annie and Greg hardly noticed. From this day forward they'd live every day on the edge, working together, loving together. Life itself was a gamble, love the biggest one of all.

Greg knew it to his soul and back. "This is forever, Annie. I love you."

"I love you." She grasped his face in her hands, hurting for every scar that ever caused him pain, cherishing each mark that had made him the man she loved. She put her hand over his heart and felt the cigarette lighter she'd given him as a wedding gift. He might not use it often, but he'd keep it near him always. She'd inscribed it with words defining their love.

While the song lasts, dance.

THE EDITOR'S CORNER

Let the fires of love's passion keep you warm as summer's days shorten into the frosty nights of autumn. Those falling leaves and chilly mornings are a sure signal that winter's on the way! So make a date to snuggle up under a comforter and read the six romances LOVESWEPT has in store for you. They're sure to heat up your reading hours with their witty and sensuous tales.

Fayrene Preston's scrumptious and clever story, **THE COLORS OF JOY,** LOVESWEPT #642 is a surefire heartwarmer. Seemingly unaware of his surroundings, Caleb McClintock steps off the curb—and is yanked out of the path of an oncoming car by a blue-eyed angel! Even though Joy Williams had been pretending to be her twin sister as part of a daredevil charade, he'd recognized her, known her when almost no one could tell them apart. His wickedly sensual experiments will surely show a lady who's adored variety that one man is all she'll ever need! You won't soon forget this charming story by Fayrene.

Take a trip to the tropics with Linda Wisdom's **SUDDEN IMPULSE,** LOVESWEPT #643. Ben Wyatt had imagined the creator of vivid fabric designs as a passionate wanton who wove her fiery fantasies into the cloth of dreams, but when he flew to Treasure Cove to meet her, he was shocked to encounter Kelly Andrews, a cool businesswoman who'd chosen paradise as an escape! Beguiled by the tawny-eyed designer who'd sworn off driven men wedded to their work, Ben sensed that beneath her silken surface was a fire he must taste. Captivated by her beauty, enthralled by her sensuality, Ben challenged her to seize her chance at love. Linda's steamy tale will melt away the frost of a chilly autumn day.

Theresa Gladden will get you in the Halloween mood with her spooky but oh, so sexy duo, **ANGIE AND THE GHOSTBUSTER,** LOVESWEPT #644. Drawn to an old house by an intriguing letter and a shockingly vivid dream, Dr. Gabriel Richards came in search of a tormented ghost—but instead found a sassy blonde with dreamer's eyes who awakened an old torment of his own. Angie Parker was two-parts angel to one-part vixen, a sexy, skeptical, single mom who suspected a con—but couldn't deny the chemistry between them, or disguise her burning need. Theresa puts her "supernatural" talents to their best use in this delightful tale.

The ever-creative and talented Judy Gill returns with a magnificent, touching tale that I'm sure you'll agree is a **SHEER DELIGHT,** LOVESWEPT #645. Matt Fiedler had been caught looking—and touching—the silky lingerie on display in the sweet-scented boutique, but when he discovered he'd stumbled into Dee Farris's shop, he wanted his hands all over the lady instead! Dee had never forgotten the reckless bad boy who'd awakened her to exquisite passion in college, then shattered her dreams by promising to return for her, but never keeping his word. Dee feared the doubts that had once driven him away couldn't be silenced by desire, that Matt's pride might be stronger than his need to possess her. This one will grab hold of your heartstrings and never let go!

Victoria Leigh's in brilliant form with **TAKE A CHANCE ON LOVE**, LOVESWEPT #646. Biff Fuller could almost taste her skin and smell her exotic fragrance from across the casino floor, but he sensed that the bare-shouldered woman gambling with such abandon might be the most dangerous risk he'd ever taken! Amanda Lawrence never expected to see him again, the man who'd branded her his with only a touch. But when Biff appeared without warning and vowed to fight her dragons, she had to surrender. The emotional tension in Vicki's very special story will leave you breathless!

I'm sure that you must have loved Bonnie Pega's first book with us last summer. I'm happy to say that she's outdoing herself with her second great love story, **WILD THING**, LOVESWEPT #647. Patrick Brady knew he'd had a concussion, but was the woman he saw only a hazy fantasy, or delectable flesh and blood? Robin McKenna wasn't thrilled about caring for the man, even less when she learned her handsome patient was a reporter—but she was helpless to resist his long, lean body and his wicked grin. Seduced by searing embraces and tantalized by unbearable longing, Robin wondered if she dared confess the truth. Trusting Patrick meant surrendering her sorrow, but could he show her she was brave enough to claim his love forever? Bonnie's on her way to becoming one of your LOVESWEPT favorites with **WILD THING**.

Here's to the fresh, cool days—and hot nights—of fall.

With best wishes,

[signature: Nita Taublib]

Nita Taublib
Associate Publisher

P.S. Don't miss the exciting big women's fiction reads Bantam will have on sale in September: Teresa Medeiros's **A WHISPER OF ROSES,** Rosanne Bittner's **TENDER BETRAYAL,** Lucia Grahame's **THE PAINTED LADY,** and Sara Orwig's **OREGON BROWN.** We'll be giving you a sneak peek at these terrific books in next month's LOVESWEPTS. And immediately following this page look for a preview of the spectacular women's fiction books from Bantam *available now!*

Don't miss these exciting books by your
favorite Bantam authors

On sale in August:
*THE MAGNIFICENT
ROGUE*
by Iris Johansen

VIRTUE
by Jane Feather

*BENEATH A SAPPHIRE
SEA*
by Jessica Bryan

TEMPTING EDEN
by Maureen Reynolds

And in hardcover from Doubleday
WHERE DOLPHINS GO
by Peggy Webb

Iris Johansen
nationally bestselling author of
THE TIGER PRINCE
presents
THE MAGNIFICENT ROGUE

Iris Johansen's spellbinding, sensuous romantic novels have captivated readers and won awards for a decade now, and this is her most spectacular story yet. From the glittering court of Queen Elizabeth to a barren Scottish island, here is a heartstopping tale of courageous love . . . and unspeakable evil.

The daring chieftain of a Scottish clan, Robert McDarren knows no fear, and only the threat to a kinsman's life makes him bow to Queen Elizabeth's order that he wed Kathryn Ann Kentrye. He's aware of the dangerous secret in Kate's past, a secret that could destroy a great empire, but he doesn't expect the stirring of desire when he first lays eyes on the fragile beauty. Grateful to escape the tyranny of her guardian, Kate accepts the mesmerizing stranger as her husband. But even as they discover a passion greater than either has known, enemies are weaving their poisonous web around them, and soon Robert and Kate must risk their very lives to defy the ultimate treachery.

"I won't hush. You cannot push me away again. I tell you that—"

Robert covered her lips with his hand. "I know what you're saying. You're saying I don't have to shelter you under my wing but I must coo like a peaceful dove whenever I'm around you."

"I could not imagine you cooing, but I do not think peace and friendship between us is too much to ask." She blinked rapidly as she moved her head to avoid his hand. "You promised that—"

"I know what I promised and you have no right to ask more from me. You can't expect to beckon me close and then have me keep my distance," he said harshly. "You can't have it both ways, as you would know if you weren't—" He broke off. "And for God's sake don't *weep*."

"I'm not weeping."

"By God, you are."

"I have something in my eye. You're not being sensible."

"I'm being more sensible than you know," he said with exasperation. "Christ, why the devil is this so important to you?"

She wasn't sure except that it had something to do with that wondrous feeling of *rightness* she had experienced last night. She had never known it before and she would not give it up. She tried to put it into words. "I feel as if I've been closed up inside for a long time. Now I want . . . something else. It will do you no harm to be my friend."

"That's not all you want," he said slowly as he studied her desperate expression. "I don't think you know what you want. But I do and I can't give it to you."

"You could try." She drew a deep breath. "Do you think it's easy for me to ask this of you? It fills me with anger and helplessness and I *hate* that feeling."

She wasn't reaching him. She had to say something that would convince him. Suddenly the words came tumbling out, words she had never meant to say, expressing emotions she had never realized she felt. "I thought all I'd need would be a house but now I know there's something more. I have to have people too. I guess I always knew it but the house was easier, safer. Can't you see? I want what you and Gavin and Angus have, and I don't know if I can find it alone. Sebastian told me I couldn't have it but I will. I *will*." Her hands nervously clenched and unclenched at her sides. "I'm all tight inside. I feel scorched . . . like a desert. Sebastian made me this way and I don't know how to stop. I'm not . . . at ease with anyone."

He smiled ironically. "I've noticed a certain lack of trust in me but you seem to have no problem with Gavin."

"I truly like Gavin but he can't change what I am," she answered, then went on eagerly. "It was different with you last night, though. I really *talked* to you. You made me feel . . ." She stopped. She had sacrificed enough of her pride. If this was not enough, she could give no more.

The only emotion she could identify in the multitude of expressions that flickered across his face was frustration. And there was something else, something darker, more intense. He threw up his hands. "All right, I'll try."

Joy flooded through her. "Truly?"

"My God, you're obstinate."

"It's the only way to keep what one has. If I hadn't fought, you'd have walked away."

"I see." She had the uneasy feeling he saw more than her words had portended. But she must accept this subtle intrusion of apprehension if she was to be fully accepted by him.

"Do I have to make a solemn vow?" he asked with a quizzical lift of his brows.

"Yes, please. Truly?" she persisted.

"Truly." Some of the exasperation left his face. "Satisfied?"

"Yes, that's all I want."

"Is it?" He smiled crookedly. "That's not all I want."

The air between them was suddenly thick and hard to breathe, and Kate could feel the heat burn in her cheeks. She swallowed. "I'm sure you'll get over that once you become accustomed to thinking of me differently."

He didn't answer.

"You'll see." She smiled determinedly and quickly changed the subject. "Where is Gavin?"

"In the kitchen fetching food for the trail."

"I'll go find him and tell him you wish to leave at—"

"In a moment." He moved to stand in front of her and lifted the hood of her cape, then framed her face with a gesture that held a possessive intimacy. He looked down at her, holding her gaze. "This is not a wise thing. I don't know how long I can stand this box you've put me in. All I can promise is that I'll give you warning when I decide to break down the walls."

VIRTUE
by
Jane Feather

"GOLD 5 stars." —*Heartland Critiques*

"An instantaneous attention-grabber. A well-crafted romance with a strong, compelling story and utterly delightful characters." —*Romantic Times*

VIRTUE is the newest regency romance from Jane Feather, four-time winner of Romantic Times's *Reviewer's Choice award, and author of the national bestseller* The Eagle and the Dove.

With a highly sensual style reminiscent of Amanda Quick and Karen Robards, Jane Feather works her bestselling romantic magic with this tale of a strong-willed beauty forced to make her living at the gaming tables, and the arrogant nobleman determined to get the better of her— with passion. The stakes are nothing less than her VIRTUE . . .

What the devil was she doing? Marcus Devlin, the most honorable Marquis of Carrington, absently exchanged his empty champagne glass for a full one as a flunkey passed him. He pushed his shoulders off the wall, straightening to his full height, the better to see across the crowded room to the macao table. She was up to something. Every prickling hair on the nape of his neck told him so.

She was standing behind Charlie's chair, her fan moving in slow sweeps across the lower part of her face. She leaned forward to whisper something in Charlie's ear, and the rich swell of her breasts, the deep shadow of the cleft between them, was uninhibitedly revealed in the décolletage of her evening gown. Charlie looked up at her and smiled, the soft, infatuated smile of puppy love. It wasn't surprising this young cousin had fallen head over heels for Miss Judith Davenport, the marquis reflected. There was hardly a man in Brussels who wasn't stirred by her: a creature of opposites, vibrant, ebullient, sharply intelligent—a woman who in some indefinable fashion challenged a man, put him on his mettle one minute, and yet the next was as appealing as a kitten; a man wanted to pick her up and cuddle her, protect her from the storm . . .

Romantic nonsense! The marquis castigated himself severely for sounding like his cousin and half the young soldiers proudly sporting their regimentals in the salons of Brussels as the world waited for Napoleon to make his move. He'd been watching Judith Davenport weaving her spells for several weeks now, convinced she was an artful minx with a very clear agenda of her own. But for the life of him, he couldn't discover what it was.

His eyes rested on the young man sitting opposite Charlie. Sebastian Davenport held the bank. As beautiful as his sister in his own way, he sprawled in his chair, both clothing and posture radiating a studied carelessness. He was laughing across the table, lightly ruffling the cards in his hands. The mood at the table was lighthearted. It was a mood that always accompanied the Davenports. Presumably one reason why they were so popular . . . and then the marquis saw it.

It was the movement of her fan. There was a pattern to the slow sweeping motion. Sometimes the movement speeded, sometimes it paused, once or twice she snapped the fan closed, then almost immediately began a more vigorous wafting of the delicately painted half moon. There was renewed laughter at the table, and with a lazy sweep of his rake, Sebastian Davenport scooped toward him the pile of vowels and rouleaux in the center of the table.

The marquis walked across the room. As he reached the table, Charlie looked up with a rueful grin. "It's not my night, Marcus."

"It rarely is," Carrington said, taking snuff. "Be careful you don't find yourself in debt." Charlie heard the warning in the advice, for all that his cousin's voice was affably casual. A slight flush tinged the young man's cheekbones and he dropped his eyes to his cards again. Marcus was his guardian and tended to be unsympathetic when Charlie's gaming debts outran his quarterly allowance.

"Do you care to play, Lord Carrington?" Judith Davenport's soft voice spoke at the marquis's shoulder and he turned to look at her. She was smiling, her golden brown eyes luminous, framed in the thickest, curliest eyelashes he had ever seen. However, ten years spent avoiding the frequently blatant blandishments of maidens on the look-out for a rich husband had inured him to the cajolery of a pair of fine eyes.

"No. I suspect it wouldn't be my night either, Miss Davenport. *May* I escort you to the supper room? It must grow tedious, watching my cousin losing hand over fist." He offered a small bow and took her elbow without waiting for a response.

Judith stiffened, feeling the pressure of his hand cupping her bare arm. There was a hardness in his eyes that matched the firmness of his grip, and her scalp contracted as unease shivered across her skin. "On the contrary, my lord, I find the play most entertaining." She gave her arm a covert, experimental tug. His fingers gripped warmly and yet more firmly.

"But I insist, Miss Davenport. You will enjoy a glass of negus."

He had very black eyes and they carried a most unpleasant glitter, as insistent as his tone and words, both of which were drawing a degree of puzzled attention. Judith could see no discreet, graceful escape route. She laughed lightly. "You have convinced me, sir. But I prefer burnt champagne to negus."

"Easily arranged." He drew her arm through his and laid his free hand over hers, resting on his black silk sleeve. Judith felt manacled.

They walked through the card room in a silence that was as uncomfortable as it was pregnant. Had he guessed what was going on? Had he seen anything? How could she have given herself away? Or was it something Sebastian had done, said, looked . . . ? The questions and speculations raced through Judith's brain. She was barely acquainted with Marcus Devlin. He was too sophisticated, too hardheaded to be of use to herself and Sebastian, but she had the distinct sense that he would be an opponent to be reckoned with.

The supper room lay beyond the ballroom, but instead of guiding his companion around the waltzing couples and the ranks of seated chaperones against the wall, Marcus turned aside toward the long French windows opening onto a flagged terrace. A breeze stirred the heavy velvet curtains over an open door.

"I was under the impression we were going to have supper." Judith stopped abruptly.

"No, we're going to take a stroll in the night air," her escort informed her with a bland smile. "Do put one foot in front of the other, my dear ma'am, otherwise our progress might become a little uneven." An unmistakable jerk on her arm drew her forward with a stumble, and Judith rapidly adjusted her gait to match the leisured, purposeful stroll of her companion.

"I don't care for the night air," she hissed through her teeth, keeping a smile on her face. "It's very bad for the constitution and frequently results in the ague or rheumatism."

"Only for those in their dotage," he said, lifting thick black eyebrows. "I would have said you were not a day above twenty-two. Unless you're very skilled with powder and paint?"

He'd pinpointed her age exactly and the sense of being dismayingly out of her depth was intensified. "I'm not quite such an accomplished actress, my lord," she said coldly.

"Are you not?" He held the curtain aside for her and she found herself out on the terrace, lit by flambeaux set in sconces at intervals along the low parapet fronting the sweep of green lawn. "I would have sworn you were as accomplished as any on Drury Lane." The statement was accompanied by a penetrating stare.

Judith rallied her forces and responded to the comment as if it were a humorous compliment. "You're too kind, sir. I confess I've long envied the talent of Mrs. Siddons."

"Oh, you underestimate yourself," he said softly. They had reached the parapet and he stopped under the light of a torch. "You are playing some very pretty theatricals, Miss Davenport, you and your brother."

Judith drew herself up to her full height. It wasn't a

particularly impressive move when compared with her escort's breadth and stature, but it gave her an illusion of hauteur. "I don't know what you're talking about, my lord. It seems you've obliged me to accompany you in order to insult me with vague innuendoes."

"No, there's nothing vague about my accusations," he said. "However insulting they may be. I am assuming my cousin's card play will improve in your absence."

"What are you implying?" The color ebbed in her cheeks, then flooded back in a hot and revealing wave. Hastily she employed her fan in an effort to conceal her agitation.

The marquis caught her wrist and deftly twisted the fan from her hand. "You're most expert with a fan, madam."

"I beg your pardon?" She tried again for a lofty incomprehension, but with increasing lack of conviction.

"Don't continue this charade, Miss Davenport. It benefits neither of us. You and your brother may fleece as many fools as you can find as far as I'm concerned, but you'll leave my cousin alone."

Beneath a Sapphire Sea
by
Jessica Bryan
Rave reviews for Ms. Bryan's novels:

DAWN ON A JADE SEA

"Sensational! Fantastic! There are not enough super-
latives to describe this romantic fantasy. A keeper!"
—*Rendezvous*

"An extraordinary tale of adventure, mystery
and magic." —*Rave Reviews*

ACROSS A WINE-DARK SEA

"Thoroughly absorbing . . . A good read and a promising new author!" —*Nationally bestselling author Anne
McCaffrey*

*Beneath the shimmering, sunlit surface of the ocean there
lives a race of rare and wondrous men and women. They
have walked upon the land, but their true heritage is as
beings of the sea. Now their people face a grave peril. And
one woman holds the key to their survival. . . .*

*A scholar of sea lore, Meredith came to a Greek island to
follow her academic pursuits. But when she encountered
Galen, a proud, determined warrior of the sea, she was
eternally linked with a world far more elusive and mysteriously seductive than her own. For she alone possessed a scroll
that held the secrets of his people.*

*In the following scene, Meredith has just caught Galen
searching for the mysterious scroll. His reaction catches them
both by surprise . . .*

He drew her closer, and Meredith did not resist. To look
away from his face had become impossible. She felt something in him reach out for her, and something in her

answered. It rose up in her like a tide, compelling beyond reason or thought. She lifted her arms and slowly put them around his broad shoulders. He tensed, as if she had startled him, then his whole body seemed to envelop hers as he pulled her against him and lowered his lips to hers.

His arms were like bands of steel, the thud of his heart deep and powerful as a drum, beating in a wild rhythm that echoed the same frantic cadence of Meredith's. His lips seared over hers. His breath was hot in her mouth, and the hard muscles of his bare upper thighs thrust against her lower belly, the bulge between them only lightly concealed by the thin material of his shorts.

Then, as quickly as their lips had come together, they parted.

Galen stared down into Meredith's face, his arms still locked around her slim, strong back. He was deeply shaken, far more than he cared to admit, even to himself. He had been totally focused on probing the landwoman's mind once and for all. Where had the driving urge to kiss her come from, descending on him with a need so strong it had overridden everything else?

He dropped his arms. "That was a mistake," he said, frowning. "I—"

"You're right." Whatever had taken hold of Meredith vanished like the "pop" of a soap bubble, leaving her feeling as though she had fallen headfirst into a cold sea. "It *was* a mistake," she said quickly. "Mine. Now if you'll just get out of here, we can both forget this unfortunate incident ever happened."

She stepped back from him, and Galen saw the anger in her eyes and, held deep below that anger, the hurt. It stung him. None of this was her fault. Whatever forces she exerted upon him, he was convinced she was completely unaware of them. He was equally certain she had no idea of the scroll's significance. To her it was simply an impressive artifact, a rare find that would no doubt gain her great recognition in this folklore profession of hers.

He could not allow that, of course. But the methods he had expected to succeed with her had not worked. He could try again—the very thought of pulling her back into her arms was a seductive one. It played on his senses with heady anticipation, shocking him at how easily this woman could distract him. He would have to find another less physical means of discovering where the scroll was.

"I did not mean it that way," he began in a gentle tone.

Meredith shook her head, refusing to be mollified. She was as taken aback as he by what had happened, and deeply chagrined as well. The fact that she had enjoyed the kiss—No, that was too calm a way of describing it. Galen's mouth had sent rivers of sensations coursing through her, sensations she had not known existed, and that just made the chagrin worse.

"I don't care what you meant," she said in a voice as stiff as her posture. "I've asked you to leave. I don't want to tell you again."

"Meredith, wait." He stepped forward, stopping just short of touching her. "I'm sorry about . . . Please believe my last wish is to offend you. But it does not change the fact that I still want to work with you. And whether you admit it or not, you need me."

"Need you?" Her tone grew frosty. "I don't see how."

"Then you don't see very much," he snapped. He paused to draw in a deep breath, then continued in a placating tone. "Who else can interpret the language on this sheet of paper for you?"

Meredith eyed him. If he was telling the truth, if he really could make sense out on those characters, then, despite the problems he presented, he was an answer to her prayers, to this obsession that would not let her go. She bent and picked up the fallen piece of paper.

"Prove it." She held it out to him. "What does this say?"

He ignored the paper, staring steadily at her. "We will work together, then?"

She frowned as she returned his stare, trying to probe whatever lay behind his handsome face. "Why is it so important to you that we do? I can see why you might think I need you, but what do you get out of this? What do you want, Galen?"

He took the paper from her. "*The season of destruction will soon be upon us and our city,*" he read deliberately, "*but I may have found a way to save some of us, we who were once among the most powerful in the sea. Near the long and narrow island that is but a stone's throw from Crete, the island split by Mother Ocean into two halves . . .*"

He stopped. "It ends there." His voice was low and fierce, as fierce as his gaze, which seemed to reach out to grip her. "Are you satisfied now? Or do you require still more proof?"

TEMPTING EDEN
by
Maureen Reynolds

author of SMOKE EYES

"Ms. Reynolds blends steamy sensuality with
marvelous lovers. . . . delightful."
—*Romantic Times on SMOKE EYES*

*Eden Victoria Lindsay knew it was foolish to break into the
home of one of New York's most famous—and reclusive—
private investigators. Now she had fifteen minutes to convince him that he shouldn't have her thrown in prison.*

*Shane O'Connor hardly knew what to make of the flaxen-
haired aristocrat who'd scaled the wall of his Long Island
mansion—except that she was in more danger than she
suspected. In his line of work, trusting the wrong woman
could get a man killed, but Shane is about to himself get
taken in by this alluring and unconventional beauty. . . .*

"She scaled the wall, sir," said Simon, Shane's stern
butler.

Eden rolled her eyes. "Yes—yes, I did! And I'd do it
again—a hundred times. How else could I reach the
impossible *inaccessible* Mr. O'Connor?"

He watched her with a quiet intensity but it was Simon
who answered, "If one wishes to speak with Mr. O'Connor, a meeting is usually arranged through the *proper*
channels."

Honestly, Eden thought, the English aristocracy did
not look down their noses half so well as these two!

O'Connor stepped gracefully out of the light and his

gaze, falling upon her, was like the steel of gunmetal. He leaned casually against the wall—his weight on one hip, his hands in his trousers pockets—and he studied her with half-veiled eyes.

"Have you informed the . . . ah . . . *lady*, Simon, what type of reception our unexpected guests might anticipate? Especially," he added in a deceptively soft tone, "those who scale the estate walls, and . . . er . . . shed their clothing?"

Eden stiffened, her face hot with color; he'd made it sound as if it were *commonplace* for women to scale his wall and undress.

Simon replied, "Ah, no, sir. In the melee, that particular formality slipped my mind."

"Do you suppose we should strip her first, or just torture her?"

"*What?*"

"Or would you rather we just arrest you, madame?"

"Sir, with your attitude it is a wonder you have a practice at all!"

"It is a wonder," he drawled coldly, "that you are still alive, madame. You're a damn fool to risk your neck as you did. Men have been shot merely for attempting it, and I'm amazed you weren't killed yourself."

Eden brightened. "Then I am to be commended, am I not? Congratulate me, sir, for accomplishing such a feat!"

Shane stared at her as if she were daft.

"And for my prowess you should be more than willing to give me your time. Please, just listen to my story! I promise I will pay you handsomely for your time!"

As her eyes met his, Eden began to feel hope seep from her. At her impassioned plea there was no softening in his chiseled features, or in his stony gaze. In a final attempt she gave him her most imploring look, and then instantly regretted it, for the light in his eyes suddenly burned brighter. It was as if he knew her game.

"State your business," O'Connor bit out.

"I need you to find my twin brother."

Shane frowned. "You have a twin?"

"Yes I do."

God help the world, he thought.

He leaned to crush out his cheroot, his gaze watching

her with a burning, probing intensity. "*Why* do you need me to find your twin?"

"Because he's missing, of course," she said in a mildly exasperated voice.

Shane brought his thumb and forefinger up to knead the bridge of his nose. "*Why*, do you need me to find him? *Why* do you think he is missing, and not on some drunken spree entertaining the . . . uh . . . 'ladies'?"

"Well, Mr. O'Connor, that's very astute of you— excuse me, do you have a headache, sir?"

"Not yet."

Eden hurried on. "Actually I might agree with you that Philip could be on a drunken spree, but the circumstances surrounding his disappearance don't match that observation."

Shane lifted a brow.

"You see, Philip *does* spend a good deal of time in the brothels, and there are three in particular that he frequents. But the madames of all of them told me they haven't seen him for several days."

Shane gave her a strange look. "You went into a brothel?"

"No. I went into *three*. And Philip wasn't in any of them." She thought she caught the tiniest flicker of amusement in his silver eyes, then quickly dismissed the notion. Unlikely the man had a drop of mirth in him.

"What do you mean by 'the circumstances matching the observation'?"

Eden suddenly realized she had not produced a shred of evidence. "Please turn around and look away from me Mr. O'Connor."

"Like hell."

Though her heart thudded hard, Eden smiled radiantly. "But you must! You have to!"

"I don't *have* to do anything I don't damn well please, madame."

"Please, Mr. O'Connor." Her tearing eyes betrayed her guise of confidence. "I-I brought some evidence I think might help you with the case—that is if you take it. But it's—I had to carry it under my skirt. Please," she begged softly.

Faintly amused, Shane shifted his gaze out toward the bay. Out of the corner of his eye he saw her twirl around, hoist her layers of petticoats to her waist, and fumble with something.

She turned around again, and with a dramatic flair that was completely artless, she opened the chamois bag she had tied to the waistband of her pantalets. She grabbed his hand and plopped a huge, uncut diamond into the center of his palm. Then she took hold of his other hand and plunked down another stone—an extraordinary grass-green emerald as large as the enormous diamond.

"Where," he asked in a hard drawl, "did you get these?"

"That," Eden said, "is what I've come to tell you."

OFFICIAL RULES

To enter the sweepstakes below carefully follow all instructions found elsewhere in this offer.

The **Winners Classic** will award prizes with the following approximate maximum values: 1 Grand Prize: $26,500 (or $25,000 cash alternate); 1 First Prize: $3,000; 5 Second Prizes: $400 each; 35 Third Prizes: $100 each; 1,000 Fourth Prizes: $7.50 each. Total maximum retail value of Winners Classic Sweepstakes is $42,500. Some presentations of this sweepstakes may contain individual entry numbers corresponding to one or more of the aforementioned prize levels. To determine the Winners, individual entry numbers will first be compared with the winning numbers preselected by computer. For winning numbers not returned, prizes will be awarded in random drawings from among all eligible entries received. Prize choices may be offered at various levels. If a winner chooses an automobile prize, all license and registration fees, taxes, destination charges and, other expenses not offered herein are the responsibility of the winner. If a winner chooses a trip, travel must be complete within one year from the time the prize is awarded. Minors must be accompanied by an adult. Travel companion(s) must also sign release of liability. Trips are subject to space and departure availability. Certain black-out dates may apply.

The following applies to the sweepstakes named above:

No purchase necessary. You can also enter the sweepstakes by sending your name and address to: P.O. Box 508, Gibbstown, N.J. 08027. Mail each entry separately. Sweepstakes begins 6/1/93. Entries must be received by 12/30/94. Not responsible for lost, late, damaged, misdirected, illegible or postage due mail. Mechanically reproduced entries are not eligible. All entries become property of the sponsor and will not be returned.

Prize Selection/Validations: Selection of winners will be conducted no later than 5:00 PM on January 28, 1995, by an independent judging organization whose decisions are final. Random drawings will be held at 1211 Avenue of the Americas, New York, N.Y. 10036. Entrants need not be present to win. Odds of winning are determined by total number of entries received. Circulation of this sweepstakes is estimated not to exceed 200 million. All prizes are guaranteed to be awarded and delivered to winners. Winners will be notified by mail and may be required to complete an affidavit of eligibility and release of liability which must be returned within 14 days of date on notification or alternate winners will be selected in a random drawing. Any prize notification letter or any prize returned to a participating sponsor, Bantam Doubleday Dell Publishing Group, Inc., its participating divisions or subsidiaries, or the independent judging organization as undeliverable will be awarded to an alternate winner. Prizes are not transferable. No substitution for prizes except as offered or as may be necessary due to unavailability, in which case a prize of equal or greater value will be awarded. Prizes will be awarded approximately 90 days after the drawing. All taxes are the sole responsibility of the winners. Entry constitutes permission (except where prohibited by law) to use winners' names, hometowns, and likenesses for publicity purposes without further or other compensation. Prizes won by minors will be awarded in the name of parent or legal guardian.

Participation: Sweepstakes open to residents of the United States and Canada, except for the province of Quebec. Sweepstakes sponsored by Bantam Doubleday Dell Publishing Group, Inc., (BDD), 1540 Broadway, New York, NY 10036. Versions of this sweepstakes with different graphics and prize choices will be offered in conjunction with various solicitations or promotions by different subsidiaries and divisions of BDD. Where applicable, winners will have their choice of any prize offered at level won. Employees of BDD, its divisions, subsidiaries, advertising agencies, independent judging organization, and their immediate family members are not eligible.

Canadian residents, in order to win, must first correctly answer a time limited arithmetical skill testing question. Void in Puerto Rico, Quebec and wherever prohibited or restricted by law. Subject to all federal, state, local and provincial laws and regulations. For a list of major prize winners (available after 1/29/95): send a self-addressed, stamped envelope entirely separate from your entry to: Sweepstakes Winners, P.O. Box 517, Gibbstown, NJ 08027. Requests must be received by 12/30/94. DO NOT SEND ANY OTHER CORRESPONDENCE TO THIS P.O. BOX.